CHRISTIANITY
IS NOT A WESTERN RELIGION

CHRISTIANITY
IS NOT A WESTERN RELIGION

Ho Jin Jun

2019

Christianity is not a Western Religion – Published by the Rev. Dr. Ashish Amos of the Indian Society for Promoting Christian Knowledge (ISPCK), Post Box 1585, Kashmere Gate, Delhi-110006.

ISBN: 978-93-88945-42-4

Laser typeset by

ISPCK, Post Box 1585, 1654, Madarsa Road, Kashmere Gate, Delhi-110006 • *Tel:* 23866323

e-mail: ashish@ispck.org.in • ella@ispck.org.in
website: www.ispck.org.in

Contents

CHAPTER - 7

CHAPTER - 8

Foreword

Dr Ho Jin Jun is one of those who contributed to the evangelical mission movement in Korea as a professor. His background of theological education is unique: he studied at Korea Theological Seminary for 7 years which is the strongest Reformed school in Korea, and he learned from the missionaries of the Orthodox Presbyterian Church in America who emphasized the self-support, self-government, and self-propagation of the Nevius Plan. He finished his Th. M in missions in Westminster Theological Seminary, established by the Orthodox Presbyterian Church.

His strong Reformed theology and missions are reflected in this book. He served the Korea World Mission Association for 5 years as the first General Secretary. He is one of the founding members of the KWMA. He spent almost his entire life in Korea involved in a teaching ministry in several schools. While he was teaching in the Asian Center for Theological Studies and the Torch Graduate School of Theology, he met many Asian church leaders and pastors in the classes and later became good friends with them. While he was teaching in a seminary, his denomination, the Korean Presbyterian Church, which is made up of the most conservative churches, called him to serve the Church as a general secretary. After he finished the work of the general secretary, he went to the mission fields of Cambodia and Myanmar to serve in seminary schools as president.

The book title he suggested may be a provocation for the Christian churches in Asia. Most Asians consider Christianity to be a Western religion. However, he attempts to defend Christianity as an Asian religion in a reasonable and logical way. His assumption is that Korean Christians do not consider Christianity as a Western religion and that the accusation of it being a Western religion is being misused in order to reject Christianity.

In chapter two, he contends that the early Asian Christian churches are responsible for Christianity becoming a Western religion. He speaks with the assumption that if early Christianity would have survived and would have been preached to the ends of Asia, Christianity would not have been accused of being a Western religion. As a Reformed missiologist, he also defends Reformation theology and mission from the criticism of other evangelicals and missions.

He highly respects the 19th century's Western evangelical missions. Many Korean missionaries and some church leaders argue that Western missions have failed in Asia except in Korea. Dr. Jun's idea is that if Western missions have failed, it should be ascribed to the stony ground for the seed of the Gospel. He severely charges Korean missions of doing money missions and project-oriented missions in the mission fields. In the nineteenth century, Western missionaries were pioneer missionaries who sowed the seed of the Gospel with tears and sacrifices in Asia. Most Korean missionaries are working on the mission fields where Western missionaries previously laid the foundation. Most nations in Asia owe much to Western missions, because hospitals, schools, and charity organizations have been established by Western missionaries, and the nationals, including non-Christians, are using them without thought to who brought them to their country. Rather, in many cases, the properties left behind the missionaries served to become the causes of church division and disputes among the church leaders. The Korean churches also have experienced this.

He discusses the present situations of the Churches in Asia from his own observation and theories of 11 years of experiences in Asia. He sincerely appeals to the churches in Asia to go back to the Bible in terms of faith, theology and mission strategy. Finally, he hopes that the churches in Asia will continuously grow and develop into mature missionary churches as a light to the Gentiles.

Rev. Yong Joong Cho Ph. D.

General Secretary, Korean World Mission Association

Preface

Christianity is an Asian religion which sprang up in Asia as a Semitic religion. The Christian gospel was first spread by Asians in Asia, then in the West. Nevertheless, the Christian population only accounts for 7% of the total population of Asia despite a long church history of 1,900 years. As a Korean student of Christian theology and missions, I attempt to examine Asian Christianity and missions by largely focusing on Southeast Asia and Korea.

In Korea, nobody condemns Christianity as a Western religion, but in Asia, Christianity is often accused and rejected as a Western religion. From the beginning, Christianity has remained a persecuted minority religion. Our assumption is that Asia is a stony ground for Christianity; this well explains the present situation of Asian missions. "Christianity is a western religion" is a common phrase used to reject Christianity among those who dislike it. In order to defend historical Christianity, I entitled the book "Christianity Is Not a Western Religion." This book, as a type of Christian apologetics, attempts to defend Christianity, something that is neglected in Asian Christian churches and theology. The apostle Peter advises the persecuted Christian Diaspora as follows: "But in your hearts revere Christ as Lord. Always be prepared to give an answer to everyone who asks you to give the reason for the hope that you" (1 Pet. 3:15).

Chapter 1 proposes that Christianity is ethnically a Semitic religion alongside Judaism and Islam, while Hinduism and Buddhism belong to the Aryan religions. The Aryans are ethnically Europeans. Our assumption is that there is a deep relation between Greek philosophy and Indian philosophy. Both the Greek culture and Indian philosophy share many commonalities.

We emphasize that Western liberalism and ideologies of communism and nationalism have contributed to making Christianity a western religion. The Korean Christians do not think that historical Christianity wore Western clothes. The arguments that Christianity failed in Asia because of Western colonies is not a plausible explanation. Japan and Thailand have not experienced western colonialism, but the Christian population is less than 1%.

Chapter 2 examines early Asian mission history from the second century until the eighth century. This chapter made a comparative study Buddhism mission and Nestorian mission in Asia, because Buddhism and Christianity moved to Asia almost at the same period, but Buddhism established many Buddhism states in Asia, but Nestorianism faded away in Asia except for in India and Syria. We briefly examined the encounter of Christianity with Mahayana Buddhism in Asia.

Our assumption is that if Christianity would have been propagated in Asia by the Asian Christian Churches, Christianity would not have been accused of a western religion. The Nestorian Churches (Nestorian) positively engaged in Asian missions as an Asian Christianity. However, Nestorian entirely disappeared in Asia with the exception of India, Syria, and Iraq. The reason for its extinction has been carefully discussed and suggested by many mission historians. The suggested reasons are: biblical messages were not preached, the Bible was not translated, they were too slow in setting up native clergy and leaders, and Christianity was misunderstood as foreign religion.

Chapter 3 is a polemic answering the criticisms that the Reformation lacked mission ventures. The Reformation laid a foundation for missionary messages and theology. The theological background of the 19th century evangelical missionary movement was more influenced by German pietism and John Wesley than Reformed theology. The first evangelical missiologist, Gustav Warneck suggested probably for the first time that the Reformation lacked in missions. Since then, many evangelical missiologists and missionaries have agreed with him. In the early 20th century, some German theologians strongly defended Luther's theology from mission perspectives. A Lutheran theologian claimed that if there were no missions in the Reformation, the modern missionary movement had no Reformation theology. The second part of this chapter is devoted to describing the mission works of the Lutheran Churches, namely John Calvin's involvement of foreign missions in a brief mission history of the Presbyterian Churches in England and America. We briefly introduce Moravian missions as the first laymen and tent making missions in world missions.

Chapter 4 defends the nineteenth century missions from the criticism that western missions has failed in Asia. In the nineteenth century, the West exported Christianity as well as secular ideologies of communism and nationalism, secular philosophy and science to Asia. Mission history tells us that many missionaries sowed the seeds of the salvation messages in Asia with tears and sacrifices; nevertheless, Christianity has only secured a foothold in Asia. A psalmist writes: "Those who sow in tears will reap with songs of joy." (Psalm 26:5), but in parts of Asia there seems to be no reaping, no songs of joy. The problem is not in its mission strategy or in western colonialism, but in Asia being a stony ground for the gospel. Western missionaries first focused on civilization mission due to the strong resistance in each nation; later they turned to evangelization by developing the self-supporting, self-propagating, and self-government principles.

Western missionaries contributed to modernization in Asia by establishing schools, hospitals and charitable organizations. India and China are proud of their long history and civilization, however, in the eyes of the missionaries there were many social evils to be abolished. In the middle of the century, mission leaders Henry and Rufus Anderson realized that civilization did not lead to evangelism and church planting; they suggested instead the so-called "three self- formula" of self-support, self-propagation and self-government.

Chapter 5 discusses the present situation of churches in Southeast Asia. This is my own observation from 11 years in Indo-China, but I try to stay as objective as possible. The Indo-China churches largely come from animistic, tribal groups and poor people. Economically, foreign dependence is an urgent issue; there is no sign of revival movement and church growth. Culturally, Indo-China is characterized by a multi-ethnic society; it even impacts the churches, so there are many ethnic-centered churches. I strongly suggest the Unreached People Movement to change their mission strategy from insisting on the use of tribal languages in evangelism to using the national language for the harmony of the multinational society. Many ideas are suggested for the churches to become a mature church.

Chapter 6 suggests early Korean missions (the early twentieth century) to be a model for churches and missions in Asia. Korean missions have been started by the American, Australian,

Canadian Presbyterians, and American Methodist missions; they organized the Korean council of evangelical missions to establish one evangelical Korean Church, but this was not accomplished. Instead, the six missions collaborated to practice the Comity System. The four Presbyterian missions successfully established one Presbyterian seminary and one Korean Presbyterian Church with their emphasis on the Bible readings and the three self-formulas of the self-support, self-propagation and self-government. The Revival movement in 1907, which greatly transformed the Korean churches, was initiated by the American missionaries.

Chapter 7 focuses on the theological confrontation between conservatism and liberalism in the Korean churches. My assumption is that the remarkable growth of the Korean churches is the outcome of conservative theology. We can say that Korean Churches are so conservative that churches have been growing to the extent of sending out more than 23,000 missionaries. The WCC ecumenical movement whose purpose was uniting the Christian churches ironically contributed to the church division in Korea. With the WCC, liberalism in the Korean Churches also served to split the churches and seminary schools. Major Korean denominations of the Presbyterians, Methodists, Holiness Churches (Korean Evangelical Church) have been divided in the conservative and the liberal groups, but it does not mean that all the local churches that belong to liberal denominations follow liberal theology. The majority of the liberal denomination still hold to evangelical faith and doctrines. In Korea, if the denomination is a member of the WCC, that church is called liberal. Theologically, this chapter discusses the theological confrontation between the conservatives and liberals by focusing on neo-orthodox theology, indigenization theology, liberation theology (Minjung theology of a Korean version of liberation theology), and pluralism theology.

Liberal theology made only impacts on seminary professors, seminary students and some intellectual Christians; most laymen were not concerned about theology. However, some radical Christian groups have had an ideological alliance with left-wing groups and pro-North Korean communists and are continuing their attack against the conservatives, Christian churches, and conservative government through mass media and public opinion.

Chapter 8 discusses how Korea, which became the first victim of the Cold War, experienced extreme confusion, poverty and corruption. However, within 4 decades, Korea economically advanced to a rich nation. Many economists and political scientists studied the reasons for economic and industrial progress in Korea and suggested their own ideas, but the answer is not simple. Some attempted to find answers in the value system of Confucianism that dominated Korean society for 500years; some try to find an answer in the education, hardworking values and allegiance of the people to the nation. Professors of social science suggest that the plural society played an important role since Korea did not have a dominant religion hindering social progress. Korea is a plural society with no state religion, no official religion, and no dominant religion. Westernization, modernization, and Christianity came together to Korea, so people never consider Christianity as Western religion. Some international mass media reports that capitalism, democracy, and Christianity played a great role in economic progress in Korea. Now, though, left-wing and socialist groups are attempting to turn upside down the established social orders and political system. We confess that Korean society is suffering an ideological conflict and clash between conservatives and left-wing groups, with evangelical Christianity continually being threatened. In conclusion, I suggest that Asian nations are to be liberated from the strong power of dominant religion, and moreover, the choice of religion should be an individual choice, not communal choice. Finally, we quote the Article 18 of the Universal Declaration of Human Rights: "Everyone has the right to freedom of thought, conscience and religion; this right includes freedom to change his religion or belief, and freedom, either alone or in community with others and in public or private, to manifest his religion or belief in teaching, practice, worship and observance."

Chapter - 1

Christianity is not a Western Religion

"Asia is a stony ground for Christianity, except for Korea!" is the title on the Korean section, reported in *The Economist* magazine dated 13 August 2014. Christianity is an Asian religion originated in Asia. However, most Asian people do not open their mind to Christianity judging that Christianity is a Western religion. Asian nations have achieved social progress by adopting western civilization and technology that partly resulted from Christianity, but they are very cold to Christians to which most nations owe their civilization and modernization. However, Asians are very hesitant to accept Christianity as an Asian religion. People go to Christian hospitals and send their children to Christian schools established by the missionaries. But if we preach the Gospel to the people on the street, they bluntly ask us, "Why should Christianity, a western religion, come to our Buddhist country? Buddhism is the best religion in the world." We need to notice that the people of the ruling class and middle class are more likely to defend their religion. We tend to suppose that intellectuals are so secular that they can be critical of the religion, but they are not so in Asia.

This shows that Christianity suffers an identity crisis in Asia. A Japanese theologian, Oki Hideo, categorizes church history into three ages: Pan-Mediterranean Age, Pan-Atlantic Age, and Pan-Pacific Age, and cites the Pan-Pacific Age as the last and the most important. In the past Pan-Atlantic Age, Christian missionaries met many cultures and religions, and had both joys and challenges. However, in the Pan-Pacific Age these days, Christian missionaries have the most difficult task ever: How can Christianity survive in Asia?

Protestant mission history in Asia has exceeded more than 200 years, but the Christian population is only 7%- 8% among the total Asian population. Even those who studied in mission schools are not hesitant to say that that Christianity is a western religion. In the West, Christianity is not downgraded by the people, however, Christianity is ignored and rejected in most Asian countries.

Several years ago, Professor Philip Hughs conducted a survey among students of McGilvary Seminary in Chiang Mai, Thailand and found that two-thirds of the students responded that the "foreignness of Christianity was a significant barrier to becoming a Christian.[1]" If we ask young students and intellectuals in Asia, how they consider Christianity, most of them would answer that Christianity is a Western religion. A famous Indian Christian, Sadhu Sunder Singh, once expressed the same words that the Christian missionaries who accompanied the British Raj still linger in the Indian mind as Western Imperialists. It has become almost fashionable among Asians to dismiss Christianity as nothing more than a Western philosophy.

We suppose that the words "Christianity is a Western religion" could perhaps win the sympathy and consent of people of other faiths in the Asian society. However, they do not recognize the fact that contradictions and inconsistencies are inherent in this statement. Buddhism is thought to be their religion, but Buddhism came to Thailand, Cambodia, Sri Lanka, and Vietnam from India. Nevertheless, Buddhism is not considered an alien religion, so why Christianity ?

The answer could be found in Asians' anti-Western and anti-Christian sentiments. Most non-Western countries were ideologically inclined to communism after World War II. Strangely, even the educated young generation does not know world history at all. Many missionaries are surprised in class that students do not know about significant historical figures such as Socrates, Alexander the Great, Ghengis Khan, and Abraham Lincoln. Communism denies world history before the Bolshevik Revolution of 1917. Since World War II, many non-Western countries, except Japan, South Korea, Singapore and Hong Kong, have joined hands with Communism ideologically. Most students in the non-Western world learned positive sides of Communism and Socialism. They did not have any information and knowledge of the free nations in the West. In Buddhist nations, students are almost forced to study Buddhism in classrooms. They do not have a chance to learn about Christianity, Capitalism, and democracy. The nationalism in Asia tends to become favorable to communism, while hostile to the West and Christianity. This has been manifested in Korea and many nations in Asia. Ironically many nationalists in Asia were educated in mission schools where many Western missionaries taught the ideology of nationalism versus western colonialism.

"Unholy alliance of Communism and Islam" is more prominent in the Muslim countries after World War II. Islam is in fact anti-democracy, anti-Western, and anti-Christianity, even though many Muslims are not so. American political scientist Daniel

Fuller defined ideological alliance of Islam and Communism as the Marx-Muhammad Pact.[2]

Many people ascribed it to the fact that the missionaries failed to identify with the people to whom they preached. We assume that is only the partial truth. As far as the accommodation and identification is concerned, Buddhist monks read and preach their scriptures in Pali or Sanskrit languages that people cannot understand. Lay Buddhists only memorize the chants, but they don't understand the meaning. In Korea, Buddhist temples have been situated on high mountains far distant from people. Very aloof from people! Nevertheless, Buddhism has been adopted in Korean society as the people's religion. It is true that the early western missionaries came to Asia almost at the same time with Western Colonialism, but we don't think that they brought western religion to plant it in mission fields. We believe that the theology of indigenization and contextualization discussed in the Madras Conference of the International Missionary Council (IMC) in 1938 rather helped Christianity to make western religion. Indigenization discussions in Madras, we put it in a word, take off western clothes from Christianity. On the other hand, we attempt to prove that Hinduism and Buddhism are Aryan (Western) religions. This assumption comes from an idea from one Indian Hindu scholar who classifies world religions into Aryan religions of Hinduism, Buddhism and Jainism, and Semite religions of Judaism, Christianity and Islam.

Aryan Origin of Hinduism and Buddhism

Many scholars have suggested that there is some relationship between Aryan as a Western Race and Hinduism as an Aryan religion. In the 19th century some Orientalists categorized world religion into Aryan religions and Semite religions. Ernest Renan, a French anti-Christian thinker, divided world religions according to race: the Aryan religion and the Semitic religion. He visited Ottoman Syria and Palestine, wrote *the Life of Jesus* in which he reduced Jesus to a simple human being claiming, "Jesus was able to purify himself of Jewish traits and, then Jesus became an Aryan." Renan considered Semite religion to be inferior to Aryan religion. So, he "elevated Jesus from the Semite to Aryan." He denied the divinity of Jesus. He is not the first one to advocate Aryan supremacy or Western supremacy over the Semite and other races.

Concerning Hinduism, Zakir Naik defines the Aryan religions as those that originated among the Aryans. These were a powerful group of Indo-European speaking people that spread through Iran and Northern India in the first half of the second millennium (BC2000 to 1500). He defines the Semitic religions as religions that originated among the Semite. According to the Bible, Noah had a son called Shem, and the descendants of Shem are known as Semites.[3] Naik refers to non-Aryan religions as Confucianism, Taoism, and Shintoism in Japan, and he claims that non-Aryan religions do not have a concept of God. They are referred to as ethical systems rather than as religions. A great American Reformed theologian Charles Hodge also understood Hinduism as an Aryan religion. He described Hinduism as follows: "There can be little doubt that when the Aryan tribes entered India, fifteen hundred or two thousand years before Christ, pantheism was their established belief. The unknown, and "unconditioned" infinite Being, reveals itself according to the Hindu system, as Brahma, Vishnu, and Shiva, — that is, as Creator, Preserver, and Restorer the endless polytheism of the Hindus naturally developed itself; and this determined the character of their whole religion."[4]

He commented in more details that "ethnologically the Hindus belong to the same race as the Greece, Rome, and other great European nations."[5] Dr. Hodge, a man of the 19th century, had a profound knowledge of Hinduism, and predicted that Hinduism would become a big challenge to Christian missions. He commented on it as follows: "The prevalence and persistency of Polytheism show that it must have a strong affinity with fallen human nature. Although, except in pantheism, it has no philosophical basis, it constitutes a formidable obstacle to the progress of true religion in world."[6]

We need to study the similarities between Indian religions and Greek philosophy including Greek religion. Recently, an Indian scholar advocated it and continues passionately his research works to prove his theory. His name is Dr. Ranajit Pal who wrote the book entitled in *the Mesopotamian origin of Buddhism*, which was also translated into Japanese in 1995[7]. He particularly challenged the first Indologist and philologist Sir William Jones who suggested that Sanskrit and Persian belong to the Indo-European languages with some similarity between Indian philosophy and Greek philosophy.

Six years ago, I visited India to interview him. Through a Korean missionary in Kolkata. I succeeded in meeting him. How did I happen to know him? In 2005 I happened to find his book in a Japanese bookstore in Tokyo. Reading the book in Japanese, I was shocked and confused. Most Buddhists and others understand that Buddha was born in Lumbini, the location of Lumbini is southern Nepal. Everybody considers Buddhism an Indian religion.

Pal insists with strong conviction that the Hindu civilization of Arian is the center of world civilization: The Aryan civilization in Persia (Iran) is the center of the Hindu and Christian civilization, accordingly Buddhism, Judaism, and Christianity came from Aryan civilization. He even claims that there is much affinities between Greek philosophy and Hindu philosophy. For him Buddhism is only derived from Hinduism. Pal highly praised and regards King Alexander as the protector and propagator of Buddhism. We cannot identify whether Alexander really knew Buddhism or not. For him the Greek civilization and Indian civilization are almost identical.

While writing this chapter, I found an interesting article which refutes the Aryan invasion of the Indian continent. This article strongly supports Pal's hypothesis. Prasad Gokhale asserts in his article that the Greeks moved westward from the Caspian Sea and settled in India. "Greeks and Egyptian derived their cosmogony from the Hindus, so the early civilization, the early arts, the indubitably early literature of India is equally the civilization of, the arts, and literature of Egypt and of Greece." According to him, Hinduism pervaded the whole Babylonian and Assyrian empires."[8] From his argument we learn that world civilization originated and spread from India to Greece and Egypt. This is really an India-centered worldview.

However, we agree that there are some affinities between Indian religious philosophy and Greek philosophy. Many scholars have already suggested evidences that there are many similarities between Greek culture and Indian culture: Sir William Jones "drew an elaborate and forced comparison between the Indian philosophical system and their supposed counterparts in the Greek schools."[9] Jones compares India with Greece: Gautama with Aristotle, Kannada with Thales, Jaimini with Socrates, Vyasa with Plato, Kapila with Pythagoras, and Patajani with Zeno. Dr. Jones lists may similarities between the two cultures. However, we want to give more emphasis to their belief system:

Greek philosophy and Indian worldview have many affinities: the body is the tomb of soul, so the soul should be liberated from the body as prison of soul. Plato had no room for the outcasts, but he keeps the order of preponderance as philosopher, warrior, and artisan. In the *Republic*, the class system is so rigid that it is almost impossible to change it.

Hinduism and Buddhism believe in reincarnation and rebirth, but they refuse physical resurrection as undesirable, because physical resurrection is only the extension of human suffering. Greek philosophy is the same in denying physical resurrection. When the Apostle Paul preached the resurrection of Jesus Christ in the Areopagus, many Athenians sneered at it. "When they heard about the resurrection of the dead, some of them sneered, but others said, "We want to hear you again on this subject." (Acts 17: 32). It is the same for Hindus and Buddhists. Physical resurrection is not the final goal of salvation. Some New Testament theologians asserted that Paul's mission in Athens was a failure. But we would not agree. Dr. F. F. Bruce rightly comments on the apostle Paul's preaching in Areopagus as follows: "At any rate, Paul had few converts in Athens; we are not told that he planted a church there. But we should remember that Athens played no part in Paul's plan of campaign, he probably did not spend more than three or four weeks there; and, for the rest, if the response to his preaching during these weeks was scanty, the fault may be sought in the Athenians rather than in Paul's messages."[10]

The dualistic worldview of matter and spirit (soul) have similarities between Greek philosophy and Indian religions. That the material world is evil does not represent typical Asian cultures. Asian culture and value system are ethic-oriented and pragmatic with loyalty to the nation and king. The material world is more important than the invisible spiritual world. Life is not *maya* (illusion), it is worthy to be enjoyed. It is not by accident that East Asian nations of China, Japan, Korea, Taiwan, and Singapore are economically more advanced than the Buddhist nations and Hindu nations. Christianity is the same in the way that the churches in Korea, China, Singapore, and Hongkong are more rapidly growing than the churches of India and South Asian nations. It is remarkable to notice that most Christians were converted from the Animistic tribal groups or ethnic people; while the Buddhists and the Hindus are very difficult to convert to Christianity.

Next, we need to discuss seriously Aryan supremacy. Unfortunately, in the nineteenth century white supremacy or Aryan supremacy began to emerge in the West, along with this came anti-Semitism and anti-Islam. Many Anglo-Saxon evangelical Christians justified the slave trade: J. Newton of "Amazing Grace" is a representative figure, even though he repented to become a pastor. Concerning this, we have an amusing example: Nikolas Ludwig von Zinzendorf (1700-1760) reported to the Danish king Christian IV that he would go to the West Indies to preach the Gospel to African slaves, the king responded with anger, "Do you really believe that it could be in the purpose of God that Negro slaves can be saved and go to heaven? You cannot possibly mean to say that with God there is no difference between race and color and that a black man is worth just as much with God as his white master? Yes, that there would in heaven be no difference between a slave and his master? You do admit, don't you, that God has indeed cursed Negroes and left them to their own to be doomed for time and eternity?"[11]

The term Aryan is derived from Sanskrit *arya*, meaning noble. The term also designates a great family of languages called the Indo-Europeans or Indo-Germanic family of tongues. During

World War II, the word "Aryan" was misused to discriminate the non-Aryan peoples by Hitler. It is Hitler who spoke openly of the superiority of the Aryan race. Hitler condemns in his book, *Mein Kampf* (My Fight) the Jews as an inferior race to be wiped out in the world.

We need to mention again Renan. He emphasized the superiority of the Aryan race over the Semite. If we quote him from Wikipedia: "Renan believed that racial characteristics were instinctual and deterministic. He has been criticized for his claims that the Semitic race is inferior to the Aryan race."[12]For Renan, the Semites were "an incomplete race." The supremacy of the Aryans led to the supremacy of Hinduism. Hindu pluralists argue that Hinduism is superior to other religions, so they have a strong conviction that "all water will eventually flow into the river of Hinduism." This is quite different from the position of Western pluralists who make all religions equal. For instance, Hindu pluralist Sarvepalli Radhakrishna, who was the most formidable Hindu opponent of Christianity and the most eloquent, learned and erudite ambassador of Hinduism all over the World, claimed that, "religions are equally true, but Hinduism, being the *Sanatana Dharma*, (the ancient religion) is the essence of them all." This attitude is being called *Hindu Philisophic Gloria* (glory of Hindu philosophy).[13]

It is important to notice that Christianity, a Semite religion, has become the white people's (Japhet) religion. Some theologians find its clue in Genesis 9:26, "May God extend Japheth's territory; may Japheth live in the tents of Shem, and may Canaan be the slave of Japheth." The Aryans are divided into the European Aryans and Asiatic Aryans. Geerhardus Vos's interpretation of Genesis 9: 26 is very interesting: "To dwell in the tents of some tribe or people is a common way of describing conquest of one tribe by another. For Japhet to dwell in the tents of Shem implies conquest of Shemitic territory by Japhetites." He even commented that this "prophecy has been fulfilled through the subjugating of Shemitic territory by the Greeks and Romans. For this blessing became one of the most potent factors in the spread of the true religion over the earth. Delitzsch strikingly remarks: 'We are all Japhetites dwelling in the tents of Shem'."[14] Vos quotes this verse to show legitimacy of Western dominance over Asians. Ellicott's commentary is the same by saying that:

While, then, it is the special blessing of Shem that through him the voice of thanksgiving is to ascend to Jehovah, the God of grace; it is Elohim, the God of nature and of the universe, who gives to Japheth wide extension and the most numerous posterities. If the most ancient civilisation and the earliest empires in Egypt and on the Tigris were Hamite, the great world- powers of history, the Chaldean, the Medo-Persian, the Greek and Roman, the Hindoo, were all Japhetic origin, as are also the modern rulers of mankind.[15]

However, as an Asian Christian, we attempt to interpret the verse Genesis 9:27 as Japhet dwells in the spiritual tent of Shem. Then what does "spiritual tent of Shem mean?" We interpret it as the Christian religion. Japhet's descendants adopted the religion of Shem, Christianity, and are blessed." European Aryans adopted Christianity as their religion and brought Christian religion to Asia. Dr. Harvie Conn interprets this verse differently from Dr. Vos by contending that: "But this hostile conquest and Japhethites overrunning Semite lands seem incongruent with the occasion of the prophecy. The concept may have in mind spiritual blessings. So, indwelling in the tents of Shem likely means dwelling as guest in the tents of a hospitable host. The idea seems rather that nations are being received into the tents of Israel to worship the God of Israel, the ingathering of the Gentiles (Eph. 3:6)."[16]

Christianity is an Asian Religion

We want to appeal to Asians that Christianity is not a Western religion, but an Asian religion. How? The main stage of the Bible is Asia, and the Bible authors are all Asians. The revelations and the histories of the Bible took place in Asia: the cultures, customs, religions, tradition and stories are related in an Asian country. The Old Testament was written in Hebrew. Even though the New Testament was written in Greek, the ministry of Jesus Christ, the stories and activities of his disciples occurred in Palestine. Geographically, Christianity originated in Asia, and first expanded in Asia, and then spread to Europe.

Many of the early Apologists and Church Fathers such as Justin, Clement, Origen, Athanasius, Tertullian, and Augustine all were Asians or Africans in their origin, even though they spoke and wrote in Latin and Greek. Nevertheless, Western Church historians made them Western theologians. The great theologian Augustine was from Carthage in Algeria. Before the civil war in 2011, Syrian Christians were very proud of the early Syrian Churches. Six Roman Popes and many theologians came from Syrian Churches, and the Syrian Churches were the center of the mission movement in the early Church. We will discuss this subject in chapter two.

What made Christianity a Western Religion?

Historically, the religions, cultural conservatives, communism, liberal theology, and enlightened thoughts are responsible for having made Christianity a Western religion. At present authoritative regimes in Asia condemn Christianity as a western religion are expelling many missionaries from their nation. The persecution of Christians in China is so serious that Christian churches in free nations deeply worry about it.

1) Christianity has been strongly resisted by other faiths , cultural conservatives and nationalists. Most world religions, including Christianity, originated in Asia. Nevertheless, the other faiths reject Christianity as a Western religion. We suppose that intentional prejudices and bias are involved by refusing religious pluralism in their society. They do not want every religion to peacefully coexist, but rather they insist that religion only wants to control and dominate their society and country. This represents the cultural policy of one religion in one nation and community. They do not know that democracy is impossible without full freedom of religion. Genuine democracy comes from pluralistic society where every religion peacefully coexists with other religions. Religious and cultural pluralism guarantees democracy of free society which the young generations are eager to enjoy in South Asia.

2) The Communists in Asia produced propaganda saying Christianity is that spy of Western colonialism and American imperialism. Historically Asia has never made ideologies of nationalism, capitalism, fascism, communism, and socialism. Nevertheless, China, North Korea, Mongolia, Vietnam, Myanmar, Laos, and Cambodia have become communist nations since the 1950s. In these countries many Christians have suffered martyrdom by the communists who contend they are spies of American imperialism and western colonial powers. Lenin once said that all religions including Christian churches are agencies of the bourgeoisie. In 1950 as soon as the Communists occupied North Korea, they began killing Christians.

Communism considers religion an opiate of the people, because religion teaches people to escape from sufferings in this world and to have their hope on another world that is life after death. It claims that religion does not inspire revolutionary fever to establish Utopia on earth. Christianity is considered the greatest obstacle to establishing an ideal Communist society. It is well-known that the Jewish-born Karl Marx showed a strong hatred towards Christianity. It is significant to note that the so-called Third World nations ideologically have shaken hands with Soviet communisms since World War II. So, their government teaches communism as an ideal to their young generations, while presenting capitalism, democracy and Christianity from negative perspectives. The dominant religion made a great impact on education in Asia, because students are required to learn only the dominate religion in schools. In Buddhist nations students learn only Buddhism, Islamic nations are the same. Most of the young generations are exposed to western secularism and western pop culture, but they do not have a chance to learn about capitalism, democracy and Christianity from a positive perspective.

3) The growing expansion of Islam encourages anti-Christian sentiment around the world. The recent increase in Muslim population and the rise of Islamic terrorism has made Christianity a target for criticism and attacks. Muslims always condemn Christianity as the religion of the Crusades. We agree that the Crusades were the biggest mistakes committed by the Roman Catholic Church, however, the Muslims do not distinguish between Catholic and Protestants. They do not recognize that they were also invaders and attackers on Christian nations. The Ottoman Turks controlled Arab nations for almost 400 years until World War I.

4) Western liberal theology made Christianity a Western religion. German liberal theologian Ernst Troeltsche who advocated the

history of religion school (*Religiongeschichtlich Schule*) boldly suggested Christian mission should not bring Christianity clothed with European dress to the mission field: "Don't preach mission, salvation and conversion, but to help the natives to elevate and raise up their spirit" (sondern vielmehr Erhebung und Aufrichting zu Hoherem im Sinn). Troeltsche said that western Christianity is a "rusted European form" (verrosteten europaischen Fommen).[17]

He denied the absolute truth claims of Christianity. Instead, he suggests elevating other religions on an equal level with Christianity. According to him, Christianity is superior to other Asian religions because Christianity was born and developed in more advanced western civilization. He rejects interpreting the New Testament solely in the light of the Old Testament, thinking that primitive Christianity was not a mere continuation of Old Testament history but had other roots such as Hellenistic Judaism, and other Oriental religions. His theology subsequently paved the way for indigenization theology, dialogue theology and pluralism theology.

The same liberal theologian Adolf Harnack put forward a thesis that Jesus and Paul did not have the idea of universalism that the gospel message should reach to the Gentiles; it is borrowed ideas from the cosmopolitanism of Hellenism. From the early 20th century, the question of the attitude of Jesus towards the Gentiles has been a debated issue, not only for students of the New Testament, but also for those engaged in foreign missions. This was due to Adolf von Harnack's massive work: *The Mission and Expansion of Christianity in the First Three Centuries*. In this book he asserts that the Christian mission to the Gentiles had been altogether outside the thought of Jesus.

The Enlightenment resulted in liberating reason from revelation and science from the bondage of Catholic Christianity.

Subsequently, sciences, the studies of religion, anthropology, and linguistics have remarkably progressed in the West. Unfortunately, secularist approaches of science negatively affect Christian theology: Biblical and historical criticism deny the inspiration and infallibility of the Bible as the outcome of ancient Asian religions and myths. W. Robert Smith (1846-1894), a professor of the New Testament in Aberdeen University, applied historical criticism to the Bible study after researching the Middle East from a cultural anthropological perspective. He was a member of the evangelical Free Church of Scotland which separated from the Church of Scotland in 1843 because of issues in relation to liberalism. The Free Church of Scotland expelled him from the University.

Canadian missiologist Don Richardson criticized the Old Testament theologian Wellhausen by arguing that "his theology based upon anthropological theory which most anthropologists no longer endorse."[18] Wellhausen was influenced by the first cultural anthropologist E. B. Tylor who insisted that Moses's monotheism evolved from polytheism. His theology is greatly impacting Asian theologians and seminary students. Tylor's theory also influenced Communist attitudes toward religions: "Tylor's view of evolutionism of religion is still taught as the main foundation of atheism in colleges and universities throughout the Communist world!"[19] Western liberal theology is Western Christianity. Lillia properly pointed out the problem of liberal theology as follows:

> Yet the liberal deity turned out to be a stillborn God, unable to inspire genuine conviction among those seeking ultimate truth. For what did the new Protestantism offer to the soul of one seeking union with his creator? It prescribed a catechism of moral commonplaces and historical optimism about bourgeois life, spiced with deep pessimism about the possibility of altering that life. It preached good citizenship and national pride, economic good sense, and the proper length of a gentleman's beard. But it

was too ashamed to proclaim the message found on every page of the Gospel, that you must change your life.[20]

If Asian Christianity is not liberated from liberal theology of the West, there may be no hope of church growth and revivals. Don Richardson who transformed head-hunting tribal people to Christians in Papua New Guinea confuted the negative effect of biblical criticism in mission fields: "The resulting school of Higher Criticism not only weakened the faith of millions of Christians and undermined the vitality of hundreds of thousands of churches worldwide, but also deflected great numbers of unbelievers from taking the Bible seriously. Yet to my knowledge no liberal scholar has ever blown a whistle and said, "Wait! Since we no longer endorse Tylor's theory, why are we still endorsing this orphaned offspring of Tylor's theory."[21]

5) The nationalist movement that emerged from Asia made Christianity a Western religion. U.S. President Wilson's nationalism fueled nationalist movements in Asia. Asian nations never made any kind of ideology such as nationalism, socialism, communism, and capitalism. Tribalism and communalism based on the same ethnic group are a priority over the nation as multi-ethnic and multi-religious communicate. Nationalism as an ideology was developed in the West, and Japan is the first country to have learned nationalism from the West. Nationalism is a spirit seeking to preserve independence and dignity of the nation. The Neo-Orthodox theologian Paul Tillich defined nationalism as pseudo-religion, and historian Arnold Toynbee once said, "nationalism is a cult of collective human power." The nationalism in Asia has been anti-western and anti-Christianity from the beginning, so it is natural that Asian nationalists condemned Christianity as western religion, and strongly appealed to their people to seeking

their identity in their religion and culture. It eventually resulted in the resurgence of Asian religions.

Concerning the relations between nationalism and religion in Asia during the 1960s, Tsumori Nakano, Japanese professor of religion and social studies, analyzed as follows:

> The emergence of nationalism and the resurgence of religion are concurrent; religion provides the identity with their people or ethnic group, it justifies discrimination and their interests by emphasizing "function of differentiation of religion." It largely dismisses fellowship and cooperation with international community. It indicates that the religion is taking control of the community of ethnic groups and contribute to strengthening the unity of their own community.[22]

It is important to notice that many nationalists in Asia were educated in mission schools where liberal missionaries taught nationalism to their students in the classroom. This is evidenced in the way that some colonial government offices accused their missionaries for instigating students to fight colonialism. We have seen that many Christian nationalists became dictators after they were elected president. They failed to apply and practice Christian ideas and values system to politics.

6) The theology of indigenization since the Madras conference in 1938 contributed to Christianity being considered a western religion. The definition of indigenization is "the act of making something more native; transformation of some service, idea, etc. to suit a local culture, especially through the use of more indigenous people in administration and employment" (Wikipedia). The definition of indigenization is that the Christian gospel needs to be preached in native languages, and the church should be planted to become self-supporting, self-governing and self-propagating. The Madras conference defined the indigenous church as follows:

"A church which rooted in obedience to Christ, spontaneously uses forms of thought and modes of action natural and familiar in its own environment" (1938 Madras Mission Conference Report II: 296).

The indigenization theology was introduced to Korea in the early 1960s, and it caused a great stir in the Korean Church: that Korean Christianity should not use "western clothes," because Christianity, which was spread by the western missionaries, wore the clothes of western culture. We do not agree with this idea: Most Korean Christians were strongly convinced that the Gospel received from the missionaries is Biblical Christianity. If it wore the dress of Greek culture, it would belong to liberal Christianity.

A Korean Christian artist dressed Jesus in traditional clothes in order to make Jesus a Korean; a liberal seminary school dressed in Confucian traditional clothes instead of western academic gowns at a graduation ceremony, and wine was replaced by traditional Korean liquor (*makkoli*) in holy communion. We don't think wine is western liquor.

The early American missionaries did not introduce western Christianity to Korea. If we summarize their gospel preached to the Koreans, "believe in Jesus to be saved from your sins." Their messages were the simple gospel in simple words for "simple people." The simple did not know theology, because at that that time most Koreans were uneducated. Korean pastors did not wear western clothes and church buildings were in Korean style. Before Korean churches learned indigenization, they already practiced indigenous principles: dawn morning prayer, The Bible woman system, layman preachers, and church buildings in a Korean style. There are many similarities between the customs and cultures of the Old Testament and Korean culture, so nobody considers the Scriptures to be western.

Asian Colonialism worse than Western Colonialism

Western colonialism has disappeared a long time ago. However, Western colonialism is being replaced by Asian colonialism: Many Asian people are experiencing colonialism by other Asians. International political scientists define it as post-Colonialism. Many ethnic minority peoples in Southeast Asia live in a new colonial era, an Asian colony. In Myanmar the Karen, Kachin and Shan ethnic minority operate their own military army to fight against the central government for their independence. The Tibetans and the Uighur refugees established their own provisional government in India and Turkey for their independence from China. The Karen have a myth about a lost book that will be returned to them by their "white brothers." In addition to this, the Karen histography documents the invasion and suppression by the Burmese. The divide-and -rule strategy of the British colonial rulers improved the status of the Karen; however, after independence, the Karen people continued fighting with the Burmese.[23] One of the most striking news in Myanmar is a conflictual issue linked to the Rakhine State crisis.

Asia cannot afford to blame Western colonialism. People in Southeast Asia say the colonies of Asians were worse than those of the West. A young general Mount Aung San of Burma and fellow nationalists have shaken the hands with the Japanese soldiers to fight to cast off British rule, but they soon realized that Japanese colonialism was worse than the British colonialism. So, again they took sides with the British. Most Asian nations are multiracial and multicultural society. Nevertheless, a dominant group and a majority religion take the initiative to suppress minority groups. Myanmar is a multiracial nation of 135 ethnic groups. In 1961, Newin's military government unilaterally declared the Burmese way to socialism, and Buddhists have a very different sense of racial superiority. The central government is heavily exploiting the resources of ethnic minorities, so minorities have armed themselves and struggle for independence. Many minority people openly claim that the Western colonies were much better than the Asian colony. Many ethnic conflicts are taking place mostly in Asia and Africa because of the discrimination and oppression by the dominant majority people.

In 1996 Rudolfo Stavenhagen, a German born Jewish Mexican sociologist, did a research on global ethnic and tribal conflicts sponsored by the UN Human Rights Commission. He listed 233 ethno-political conflicts classified as follows: 81 groups are ethno-nationalists, pursuing some type of separatist objective; 45 groups are described as ethno-classes who demand more equitable treatment; 83 ethnic groups are concerned about their autonomy, and 49 ethnic groups have religious issues involved. 66 ethno-political groups are classified as communal issue who seek power for them.[24] In Southeast Asia religions do not play the role of reconciliation in the ethnic conflict, rather contributing to deepen the conflicts among the majority and the minority groups. Ooi Keat suggested that: "Religious themes are sometimes closely connected to issues of land management and ethnic diversity. In mainland Southeast Asia there are four countries – Myanmar, Thailand, Laos, and Cambodia –in which the predominant religion is Theravada Buddhism. Even in countries where several religions are recognized by the state, it is common to hear the mantra that "To be (Lao, Thai, Bamar, etc.) is to be Buddhist. This issue is particularly sensitive as religious affiliation is one notable aspect that marks ethnic groups as minorities. Some surmise that the willingness to emphasize religious differences reflects the determination minority groups to break away from the majority population that dominate the state."[25]

We defended that Christianity is an Asian religion, not a Western religion. An anti-Christianity, anti-Western Colonialism and Asian religions accuse Christianity of a Western religion. In addition to this, liberal theology and ideology contributed to making Christianity a Western religion. Asians blame Western Colonialism, but some Asian nations are facing a new colonialism by the same Asians. The ethnic conflicts in South East Asia show this. We are living in an age of pluralism, so the pluralists in Asia and the West dismiss the negative aspect of Asian religions. For Asia to be a genuine pluralistic society, the rights of minority people and freedom of religion should be guaranteed. Pluralists need to hear the voice of an Indian mission leader who has experienced a negative side of Asian religion:

> In Asia the religion of Babylon is woven into every waking minute of the day. Without Christ, people live to serve demon spirits. Religion relates to everything including your name, birth, education, marriage, business deals, contracts, travel and death. Because Oriental culture and religion are a mystery, many people in the West are fascinated by it without knowing the power of these demons to blind and enslave their followers. What routinely follows the mystery religions of Babylon is degradation, humiliation, poverty and suffering- even death.[26]

Endnotes

[1] Kelly Hildebrand, "A historical analysis of hindrance related to the slow growth of Christianity in Thailand," http://www.academia.edu/37250138: December 4, 2018.

[2] Graham E. Fuller, *A World Without Islam* (New York: Little Brown, 2010), 224-25.

[3] Dr. Zakir Naik, "Categorization of Major World Religion," https://www.islam101.com/religion/categoriesofReligion

[4] Charles Hodge, *Systematic Theology*, vol. I, (Grand Rapids: Christian Classics Ethereal Library, 2005), 199.

[5] Charles Hodge, 242.

[6] Charles Hodge, 243.

[7] Ranajit Pal, *Butkyono Mesopotamian Kikigensetz* (*The Mesopotamian Origin of Buddhism*) (Osaka: Dongbang Pub., 1995).

[8] Prasad Gokhale, "Antiquity and Continuity of Indian History" (1996) *www.gaurang.org/indian_phil/prasad_gokhale_indian_history.html*

[9] DuckDuckGo, "Ancient Greek philosophies, Buddha's Philosophy, and Vedic philosophies?" https//www.quora.com/What-are-the-smilarities-and-differences-between-the-ancient-Greek-philosophiles-Buddha. December 11, 2018.

[10] F. F. Bruce. *Commentary on the Book of the ACTS* (Grand Rapids: Eerdmans, 1976), 365.

[11] Brother Andrew, *Battle for Cry* (Old Tappan: Fleming H. Revel, 1997), 60.

[12] "Ernest Renan," https://en.wikipedia.org/wiki/Ernst_Renan: December 10, 2018.

[13] Ho Jin Jun, *Religious Pluralism and Fundamentalism in Asia* (Colorado Springs: International Academic Pub., 2002),

[14] Geerhardus Vos, *Biblical Theology: Old and New Testaments* (Grand Rapids: Eerdmans, 1948), 58-59.

[15] https://biblehub.com/commentaries/genesis/9-27.htm

[16] Harvie M. Conn, "God's Plan for Church Growth: An Overview," in *Theological Perspectives on Church Growth*, ed., Harvie M. Conn, (Nutley, New Jersey: Presbyterian and Reformed Pu., 1976), 4.

[17] Heinrich Balz, "'Uberwindung der Religionen' und das Ziel der Mission: Die Diskussion zwischen G. Warneck und E. T. Troelztch 1906-1908," in *Es began in Halle,* eds Dieter Becker/Andreas Feldtkeller, Heraus, (Erlangen: Verlag der Ev.-Luth. Mission, 1997), 109.

[18] Don Richardson, *Eternity in Their Hearts* (Venture, California: A Division of Gospel Light, 1981), 142.

[19] Don Richardson, 146.

[20] Mark Lilla, *The Stillborn God: Religion, Politics, and the Modern West* (New York: Alfred A. Knopf, 2007), 301.

[21] Don Richardson, 142.

[22] Nakano Tsmori, Iita Takamimi, and Yamanaka Hirosi, eds., *Shyukyoto nashonalizumu* (Religion and Nationalism), (Kyoto: World Thought Pub., 1999), 18-24.

[23] Ooi Keat and Volker Grabowsky, *Ethnic and Religious Identities and Integration in Southeast Asia* (Chiang Mai: Silkworm, 2017), 62.

[24] Rodolfo Stavenhagen, *Ethnic Conflicts and the Nation-State* (New York: St. Martin Press, 1996), 11.

[25] OokiKeat and Volker Grabowsky, 14.

[26] K. P. Yohanan, *Revolution in World Missions* (Lake Mary, Florida: Creation House, 1996), 161.

Chapter - 2

Early Christian Missions in Asia

Christian church history has largely been written by western scholars, so Asian church history has not been much of a concern for them. Dr. Samuel Moffett's, *A History of Christianity in Asia,* has practically become the textbook for those who study Asian church history. Western church historians write of great theologians such as Clement, Oregon, Athanasius, Tertullian, Cyril, and Augustine as western theologians, but most of them were born in Asia and North Africa. Cyprian, Tertullian, and Augustine were born in North Africa, and Justin the Martyr and Apologist was born in current Palestine. However, Moffett calls Tertullian and Augustine great Western theologians.[1] In response to this, Professor Claude Lepelley properly points out that "Western Christianity was not born in Europe but south of the Mediterranean."[2]

The study of the early Asian church is not easy, due to the lack of reliable materials. A church historian, L. W. Brown also argues that, "The history of Asian Christianity from the second to the sixteenth centuries is recognized firstly as a complex of stories and images. They portray the actions of individuals or of movements, personal experience or socio-political forces."[3] In Asian history it is often difficult to make distinctions between myth and history.

This chapter deals with Buddhist missions in Asia for several reasons. First, Buddhism and Christianity moved to Asia almost at the same period, but Buddhism was established in many nations, Nestorianism faded away in Asia except for India and Syria.

Secondly, Buddhism and Nestorianism were generally accepted in nations where Animism (Shamanism) was predominant. In regard to Buddhism, Kenneth Latourette pointed out that Buddhism never displaced an advanced religion in any nation in Asia. This shows that Buddhism failed to attract followers from among the people of developed civilization or advanced religion.[4] Buddhism and Nestorianism gained many followers in Shamanistic Mongolia. Even at present the Christian churches in Asia are generally growing in animistic tribal groups or minority group. Because of this, it is hardly expected for Christians to transform their nation.

Thirdly, the two religions have shared the same experience in which their nations have been taken over by Islam; Syria, Jordan, Egypt, and Ethiopia were Christian nations before the Muslim conquest. Indonesia (Java island) and Malaysia were once Buddhist nations, but now have become Islamic nations since the ninth century. Uighur was half Buddhist and half Christian before the eighth century. There were many Nestorian Christians in Central Asia, however, it has now become very Islamic.

Fourthly, both Buddhism and Nestorianism are foreign religions imported from India and Syria, respectively. However, Buddhism is never regarded as a foreign religion in any nation of Asia, while Nestorian is regarded as foreign religion in India and China.

Fifthly, many nations which Buddhism and Nestorianism reached overlap, namely India, Persia, Central Asia, Thailand, Myanmar, Laos, Cambodia, Sri Lanka, Tibet, China, Japan and South Korea. Buddhism is an official and dominating religion in Thailand, Myanmar, Cambodia, Sri Lanka, Tibet, Mongol, and Japan. In Korea, China, and Nepal, Buddhism is the religion of the majority. However, Nestorian churches did not survive in these countries.

Sixthly, both Buddhism and Nestorianism develop and encourage an ascetic life. Even today Buddhist monks in Southeast Asia have only two meals a day. In China, Chinese were familiar with the monasteries established by Nestorians because Buddhism had established many monasteries as well during the Tang Dynasty. "The Christianity of China seems to have been in the main monastic – a characteristic by no means detrimental in a country so familiar with the traditions of Buddhist monasticism."[5]

Buddhist Missions in Asia

We can summarize the characteristics of Buddhist missions as follows: Buddhism has been propagated without many missionaries from India. For example, a Buddhist royal son of India married the royal daughter of Cambodia; Buddhism thus automatically became the state religion of Cambodia around the 2nd century C.E. The king of Cambodia adopted Buddhism as the state religion for national defense and prosperity, desiring for his nation to maintain national and communal solidarity. Buddhism was syncretized with animism or folk religion in every nation it reached. The common Buddhists are more interested in blessings, health, and fortunes through animistic practices of prayer and donations to monks and temples. Generally, the people in Buddhist nations become Buddhist without knowing Buddhism. *"In Buddhist Nations there is no Buddhism.*" This is the title of the book I wrote in 2009 in Cambodia. How then did Buddhism become a state religion or a dominating religion in Asia? The answer is to be found not in the mission strategy of Buddhist missions, but rather in Asian cultures in which community or groups take precedence over the individual. Buddhism is a communalistic and collective religion. On the other hand, Christianity is an individualistic religion encouraging the rights of individual.

Basic to Buddhist teaching is the need to escape, to be liberated, from the world. Enlightenment is a fundamental teaching of Buddhism. The meaning of "enlightenment" is that the human can reach mystical union with Nirvana which is "Ultimate Reality." As we carefully examine Buddhism, Buddhism seems to be an individualistic religion. But the "Ultimate Reality," which is also called "Nirvana" or "Nibbana," to which most Buddhists strive to reach through meditation or other designated ways, is an impersonal being, or a cessation of existence. Individual could not exist in Nirvana, only invisible Totality. This is the most important worldview of Buddhism. The communalism or collectivism of Buddhism has been misused in the horrible history of the Killing Fields in Cambodia in 1975-1978.

Pol Pot, was responsible for having killed more than 2 million Cambodians, nevertheless, he justified his cruel mass killing by adopting the Buddhist teachings. He contended that the greatest sin in Buddhism is to affirm oneself. An individual must be absorbed into the universe of the Totality or the Whole. Pol Pot interprets this as, "there is no individual in Nirvana, only invisible Totality." Pol Pot specialist Philip Short explains how Pol Pot used Buddhist doctrines in order to mobilize the poor young men in Cambodia. He cunningly used Buddhism to achieve his political ambition. Philip Short properly explains it: "Theravada

Buddhism is intensely introspective. The goal is not to improve society or redeem one's fellow men; it is self-cultivation, in the nihilistic sense of the demolition of the individual. The grammar of Theravada Buddhism permeated Khmer communists thought, just as Confucian notions helped to fashion Maoism."[6] From these words, we can easily find a Buddhist tincture in Pol Pot. Several Buddhist scholars already compared nirvana with a vast sea. An individual going into nirvana is explained as a dewdrop falling down into the sea disappearing into a calm, windless sea. Based on these teachings, the Khmer Rouge attempted to convince Cambodians to think of themselves not as individuals, but as part of the overall collective. Communism created many slogans by which they attempted to dehumanize Cambodians, representing individuals as mere cogs in a revolution and convincing them to give up their souls for the glory of the *Angkar* (Khmer Rouge government).[7]

Buddhist missions in Asia are similar to Roman Catholic missions in the Medieval age in which the king's religion become the people's religion (*cuius regio, eius religio*). In this regard Buddhism was propagated from the top down. King, rulers and people accepted Buddhism as their religion, thus the king became a guardian or protector of Buddhism. Persecution in the expansion of Buddhism is unheard of in Asia. Why did kings and rulers initiate the acceptance of Buddhism? Kings wanted Buddhism to teach ethics and morals to their people, and through Buddhism attempted to unite their nations as well as consolidate their political power. This indicates that Buddhism functions as a political ideology for both nation and community. In the middle of the 3rd century B.C., for example, Ashoka the Great who was an Indian emperor of the Maurya Dynasty (268-232 BCE) adopted Theravada Buddhism as the state religion and sent missionaries to Sri Lanka, Egypt and even to Greece for the expansion of Buddhism world-wide. In this respect, royalty and Buddhism constituted a symbiotic relationship in Theravada Buddhist nations. Theravada Buddhism functions to legitimatize the king as a god, and in return the king provides special privileges to the religious elite and their temples. Sri Lanka, Thailand and Myanmar have a proverb stating that there is no country without Buddhism.

Encounter of Christianity with Buddhism

In this chapter we will discuss the encounter of Christianity with Buddhism in Asia. In the early twentieth century it was suggested by some theologians that when Christianity encountered Buddhism in India and China in the second century, it eventually resulted in impacting Buddhism, especially Mahayana Buddhism. A Jesuit Father, Joseph Dahlmann (1861-1930), an expert on Indian religions and Sanskrit language, proposed a challenging argument provoking Buddhists that intercommunication occurred in the second century between Christianity and Buddhism in India, and that it helped change Mahayana Buddhism into a "pseudo-Christian form."

Latourette also agreed with the proposed theory that Mahayana Buddhism has become a modified version of Christianity by adopting some doctrines and teachings of Christianity.[8] Allen Clark, an early American Presbyterian missionary who discovered many similar teachings and doctrines between Christianity and Mahayana Buddhism, made a conclusion that the concept of the eternal god, the Savior Buddha, the redemption, the coming of Messiah Buddha, the doctrine of heaven and hell are not original Buddhist teachings, but are borrowed ideas and doctrines from Christianity. This kind of assumption is found in Karl Barth's *Church Dogmatic.* He devoted more than 40 pages to the description of "Pure Land Buddhism" (Zen Buddhism) in Japan. He focused on a particular pure Land Buddhism in Japan and, interestingly, described it as "Japanese Protestantism." He called it, "the most adequate and comprehensive and illuminating heathen parallel to Christianity in the Pure Land Buddhism founded by Genku Honen in the twelfth century." Barth discussed the striking parallel to the truth of Christianity and suggested the possibility of contacts between these two religions in China or elsewhere in Asia.[9]

The Catholic Church

The apostolic Christian faith was continued by the Catholic Church, which emerged in the second century. Dr. Walker, a church historian, defines the early Christian Church as the Catholic Church, denoting that the Christian churches held firm to the apostolic faith and doctrines. To him, this church is the most ideal and pure church that has existed in history. This church is unrelated to Roman Catholicism. Walker expresses it clearer: "Neither Gnosticism nor Monasticism, though extremely perilous, were ever embraced by a majority of Christians. The large churches remained faithful to historic Christianity. By the latter third of the second century it was calling itself the "Catholic" Church. The word "Catholic" was first used by Ignatius, who employed it in the Platonic sense of "universal" as opposed to the particular. It is next to be found in the letter of the Church of Smyrna, describing the martyrdom of Polycarp (156)."[10] The early Christians shared a common belief, a relatively simple model of worship, strict moral principles, locally-centered supervisory bishops, a close relationship of saints in a local church, and a sacred ceremony. At that time, the local bishop exercised his authority with loose church organizations, and the directors filled leadership positions as a group. Those who did not accept the confession of faith and church service were not allowed to attend the service.

England's historian Edward Gibbon (1737-1795) highly regarded the early Christian churches as the virgin purity of the church. He was very negative to Roman Catholicism, so his book has been prohibited by the Vatican for a long time. He highly regards the early Christian Churches and the believers as follows: "It has been remarked, with more ingenuity than truth, that the virgin purity of the church was never violated by schism or heresy before the reign of Trajan or Hadrian, about one hundred years after the death of Christ. We may observe, with much more propriety, that, during that period, the disciples of the Messiah indulged in a freer latitude both of faith and practice than has ever been allowed in succeeding ages."[11]

Ralph Winter emphasized in the class that the early 300 years of Christian missions exceeded the one thousand years of the Roman Catholic missions. It indicates that the early Christian churches had spiritual vitality and moral purity in the midst of severe persecutions and sufferings. Every believer of the early churches confessed their apostolic faith in a baptism ceremony: "Do you believe in Jesus Christ the Son of God, who was born of the Holy Spirit and the Virgin Mary, who was crucified under Pontius Pilate and died, and rose and the third day living from the dead, and ascended into heaven, and sat down at the right hand of the Father, and will come to judge the living and the dead." "I believe." Do you believe in the Holy Spirit, and the Holy Catholic Church, and the resurrection of the flesh?" "I believe."[12]

The Syrian Church

If Syria is the cradle of the world civilization, the Syrian Church is the birthplace of the Christian missions. Edessa was also a mission center with the city of Antioch. Thomas, a disciple of Jesus Christ, was sent to India. It is a popular belief that Thomas planted the Church in India, despite a lack of historical evidence. The Thomas Churches are said to be the pride of the Indian Christians as well as for the people of other faiths in India. Indian president Rajendra Prasad, a devout Hindu, once said that the Indian Church planted by Mar (saint) Thomas is older than that of Europe, and it is a pride of all Indians. The Syrian Church developed a monastery along with the Egyptian churches. Nestorius, the founder of Nestorian, studied in a monastery in Syria. In Antioch and Edessa, the schools were established with strong focus on spiritual discipline, Bible study, and mission. These schools had over a thousand students in the sixth century. The Syrian Church produced great theologians such as Chrysostom and Theodosius who influenced Nestorius. Before the Arab Spring of 2011, there were more than 3 million Christians in Syria among the 2,300 million total population. The Syriac Orthodox Church which still dominate churches in Syria traces its history to Peter and Paul. The Syriac Orthodox Church is one of the Oriental Orthodox churches along with the Coptic Orthodox and the Armenian Orthodox churches.

Theologically, the Eastern Churches rejected the Christology of the Chalcedon Council (451). The Eastern Churches comprised the Oriental Orthodox Church (the Syrian Orthodox Church), the Coptic Orthodox and the Armenian Orthodox as different from the Greek Orthodox Church (the Byzantine Orthodox). Chalcedonian Christology is that Christ is one person in two natures of full humanity and full divinity. Jesus Christ is *Deus et Homo* (God and Man). But the Oriental Orthodox Church (Nestorian) holds that Christ is one nature --the Logos Incarnate of the full humanity and full divinity. This is the doctrinal difference which separated the Oriental Orthodox Churches from the rest of Christendom. It eventually resulted in a long time of struggle between those who accepted the Chalcedon and those who rejected it.[13] Later the Churches who rejected the Chalcedon Council were severely persecuted from the Byzantine Orthodox Church and they fled to Persia which contributed to church growth and missions in Persia. The Persian Churches became the missionaries sending churches in Asia with the Syrian Church.

The Syria Orthodox Church attributes their origin to Paul and Peter. However, they failed to continue the Apostolic faith and doctrines as well as the faith and theology of the Catholic Church. This has been manifested in the theologians of the Syrian Church such as Ephraem, Bardesane, and Afraate (Aphraates). They were representative theologians of the Syrian Churches. Dr. Crawford Burkitt who deeply studied early Syrian Christian theology concluded that the theology of Syrian theologians is much different from the apostolic tradition and the confessions and theology adopted at the Christian Councils of Nicaean and Chalcedon, etc. According to him, the theological explanations and rhetoric of the Syriac-speaking theologians are not in conformity with the apologists Justin Martyr and Tertullian who defended Christian truths against the accusations and condemnations of pagan philosophers. The Syrian theologians wrote theological books, commentaries, sermons, and doctrines generally in poetic and imaginative, not philosophical and apologetical. For example, Afraate compared the Church of Christ to a building which was made of materials of various colors, and described the Holy Spirit as the "Mother of Christ" and the "Queen of the Heaven."[14] F. Crawford Burkitt criticized Ephraim, saying that "it is really very difficult to extract from Ephraim any clear exposition of his views. He goes on from symbol to symbol, and the points he emphasizes are sometime striking, sometime preposterous, but always fanciful."[15]

Dr. Crawford is also very negative to the theology of Ephraim. He wrote many pages to explain the writings and articles of the early Syrian theologians. We quote Ephraim from Crawford: "The touch of piety and mysticism in this informal peroration should incline us, I think, to judge leniently of S. Ephraim's feeble philosophy and fanciful argumentation. But the philosophy is indeed very feeble and the argumentation excessively feeble. . . Without the Creeds I cannot but help fearing that the theology of Ephraim might have led the Syriac-speaking Church into Tritheism."[16] The explanations of the Trinity are too much fanciful and allegory. For instance, "Father clothes him with armor, the Son makes him grasp the shield, the Spirit helps him in the contest." This kind of sentences may not be heretical; but they are worse. This rhetoric in theology holds a danger of leading to superstition.

Nestorian Missions

Nestorius (386-450), Patriarch of Constantinople from 428-43, was condemned as heretical at the Council of Ephesus in 431 and at Council of Chalcedon in 451. This resulted in the Nestorian schism. In Persia, the churches who follow Nestorianism were called the Church of the East. Nestorian declared its independence from western Christianity in 424. Unfortunately, the vision of one holy, catholic (universal), and apostolic Church has been broken. "I believe in one holy, catholic, and apostolic Church" (*Credo unam sanctam catholicam et aposotolicam ecclesiam*) is a common confession of Roman Catholics and Protestants. In regard to this, Nestorianism specialist John England comments as follows:

> This growth of an autocephalous church with its distinct theology, along with the political isolation enforced by the ideology of the west, would ensure that the Church of the East developed independently of Constantinian Christianity. Nestorian emphasis upon such doctrines as the humanity of Jesus strengthened this

independent development to provide the preconditions for specific Iranian Christianity of a markedly anti-ascetic character.[17]

However, the Nestorianism condemnation is still controversial in church history, because many theologians do not agree with it. Dr. Paul Pierson, from whom I learned mission history at Fuller Seminary, argues as follows: "His Christology was probably orthodox, although perhaps not stated adequately. Ecclesiastical politics were also involved. The controversy was a factor in the breach between the East and the West, and the church in Persia became Nestorian."[18] In Church history an unfortunate incident occurred in the seventh century when the Muslims invaded the nations now known as the Arab nations, the birthplace nations of Christianity. Church history tells us that the Asian Christians who have been threatened by the Muslims asked the Western Christians to help them, however, the Western churches ignored the heartfelt cry for help. I myself visited a small Christian community in Egypt that was surrounded by strong, thick wall with a small, narrow door in an effort to protect themselves from the threat of the Muslims. If Western Christianity would have mobilized the Crusaders to help the suffering Asian Christians at that time, we imagined that world history would have entirely changed.

I happened to have an interview with a leader of the Middle East Council of Churches twelve years ago. The organization is a union organization of the many Orthodox and Protestant churches in the Middle East, cooperating with the WCC. He told me that the same ecumenical conferences involving the Nicean and Chalcedon's theological decisions that condemned Arius and Nestorius were political, cultural and theological factors on the side of Western Christianity. "Arius and Nestorius are not heretical." He appealed to me that Western Christians should not be prejudiced by the Middle East churches. They do not like to be called "old church," "separate church," or "heterogenous church." "We seven million of Christians in the Middle East are so diverse in doctrines, rituals and worship style that it is not simple to be generalized into a simple category."

Nestorian sent many missionaries to countries of Asia: from Persia, Arabia, India, Central Asia, China, Cambodia, Vietnam, Japan, and Korea. The missionaries of C&MA in Vietnam and Cambodia have published many papers and articles in their seminars, arguing that Nestorianism arrived in the Southeast as early as the fifth century. Their assumptions are based on the folk tales and oral traditions in which there are similar stories like the creation and floods in the Genesis. From about the end of the second century until the beginning of the fourteenth, Nestorianism was noted for its missionary zeal. Indeed, the difficulty is to find a place in all Asia where Nestorian Christians or missionaries have not gone. Some Church historians claim that Nestorianism came to Japan before the close of the eighth century.

In 635, it is believed that Nestorian missionaries arrived in China out of which Nestorianism then came to Korea and Japan. That assumption has not yet proved by the scholars. The Nestorian monument standing in a corner of Xi'an City demonstrates that Nestorianism flourished during the seventh century. It is true that many Christian symbols of Maria, images, and crosses had been found in the Buddhist statues, architect, and stones of Buddhism temples. Some Christians groups are still "digging ditches" to discover them. Nestorian is believed to have "spread through merchants, accountants, bankers, and physicians, as well as missionaries, monks and priests and in some cases, women who married chiefs of central Asian tribes."[19]

Why did Nestorianism fade away?

Our main concern is, why did Christianity fade away in Asia? "Nestorianism disappeared entirely, as if it had been wiped out with a sponge." These are   the words of a famous Canadian missionary, Dr. James Gale told to American missionary J. Gordon Holdcroft a specialist on   Nestorian missions. If Christianity had survived and spread to every nation of Asia by the Asians, it would not have appeared to be a Western religion. An extreme criticism came from a Scotland Church historian John Stewart on the failure of Nestorian missions. He said, "There is a lot of history of the transfer, but there was no spiritual revival movement through the Bible. The ordinances and the Lord's Supper have developed, but have there been Bible-centered sermons?.[20]Even he relates the appearance of the fearful Muslim powers in the Arab world with the failure of Nestorianism, claiming: "The rapid incursions of Islam into Persia, Syria and central Asia must no longer be looked upon as the impact of an entirely new set of ideas. The way for its triumph had been prepared from the first through the expansion and then through the failure and decadence of Nestorian Christianity."[21] In addition to this, we assert that true Christianity was not propagated in Arabia at the time of Muhammad. Edward Gibbon correctly pointed out the same:

> The Christians of the seventh century had insensibly relapsed into a semblance of paganism; their public and private vows were addressed to the relics and images that disgraced the temple of the East; the throne of the Almighty was darkened by a cloud of martyrs, and saints, and angels, the objects of popular veneration; and the Collyridian heretics, who flourished in the fruitful soul of Arabia, invested the Virgin Mary with the name and honours of a goddess. The mysteries of the Trinity and Incarnation appear to contradict the principle of the divine unity. In their obvious sense they introduce three equal deities, and transform the man Jesus into the substance of the son of God; . . .and each of Oriental

sects was eager to confess that all, except themselves, deserved the reproach of idolatry and polytheism. [22]

From the above quotation we read the Collyridian which is an unfamiliar word for us. "Collyridianism was an alleged Early Christian heretical movement in pre-Islamic Arabia, whose adherents apparently worshipped the Virgin Mary, mother of Jesus, as a goddess"(Wikipedia). Various reasons for the extinction of Christianity have been suggested in many ways. Moffett raises the question of how the churches in Asia have become extinct: "Why did Asian Christianity come so near to extinction just as Christianity of the West was about to circle the globe? What differences, East and West, between the character of the Christians, or the nature of their faith, or the structure of their churches, or the social and political environment in which they grew or declined led to such surprisingly contrary consequences on the two continents?"[23]

We think that Asian churches need to learn from Dr. Moffett. He has served in Korea for several decades as a missionary and scholar. When he was the president of Asian Center for Theological Studies (ACTS), I was also a professor of Mission at that school. Dr. Moffett is very familiar with the churches in Asia. He gave valuable advice and lessons to the Asian Christian community. We summarize Moffett's explanations on the failure of Christianity in Asia. First, he refers to the geographical isolation of the Christians widely dispersed in many places of Asia; consequently, they could not have communication and fellowship with other Christian communities. Rome to London, for example, is only about a thousand miles. But in Asia in the church's Persian period to travel from the Nestorian patriarch's seat in Seleucia-Ctesiphon to China was a journey of more than five thousand rough, winding, and frightening miles. Geographical isolation prevented from the Nestorian churches becoming an effectively cohesive continental community. The second factor is numerical. The Christian population in Asia was smaller than in Europe. Oriental Asian Christianity never planted a large enough critical mass of Christians in any Asian national culture sufficient to change the course of its history as decisively as Catholicism and Orthodoxy changed Europe. The third reason is that the harsh oppression and severe persecution caused Christians in Asia to become extinct. In the fourth century the numbers of Christian martyrs in Persia surpassed the numbers of martyrs in the Roman Empire for three hundred years. After the Mongol Empire, who were tolerant to Christianity, Tamerlane, the king of the Timur Empire was given the name of the "exterminator" of Christians in Asia for his wholesale massacres of the Christians. The fourth factor was the encounter of Christian religion with Asian religions and culture. Moffett states it as follows: "The pagan religions of the West were already crumbling when Christianity entered Europe, but in its birthplace, Asia, religion constituted a formidable obstacle to Christian expansion. Its missionaries met head-on some of the most powerful religions the world has known Persian Zoroastrianism, Indian Hinduism, Chinese Buddhism, Confucianism, and Arab Islam. Not surprisingly they resisted."[24]

In Asia, the persecution was so severe that Christianity almost didn't survive. Zoroastrianism of Persia and India, Buddhism of Southeast Asia, Islam of the Middle East, Hinduism of India, and folk religions of each country horribly oppressed Christianity. In Mongolia alone, Nestorian Christians were once protected by kings and nobles, but when a Christian or protected king stepped down, the next king or powerful man oppressed and persecuted them. The hardest persecution was from Tamerlane of the Timur Empire. He slaughtered tens of thousands of believers and dissidents in

his own country and in India. The word Tamerlane was used by
Christians in early Asia, meaning "dried man."

The fifth factor was that the churches in Asia were not protected
by the political powers. Asia never produced a Constantine. That
was the pivotal difference between Asian and European Christian
history. Dependence upon the political power is always perilous
to religious integrity and is not an unfamiliar phenomenon in
Western church history. During the almost two hundred years
of the Mongol Empire, Nestorianism had been favored by
the daughter-in-law of Genghis Khan, Sorakaktani and some
princes. Sorakaktani became a mother of Kublai Khan the first
King of Won Dynasty (1215-1294) and was a devout Nestorian
Christian, but Kublai Khan and other princes did not convert
to Nestorian. The sixth reason is the ethnic introversion of the
churches in Asia. Nestorianism failed to meet the intellectual
debates from the national intellectuals and, from the pressures of
religious discrimination, they entered into their own ghettos. The
more serious problem was that Christianity was misunderstood
as a Syrian or Persian religion in India and China, because the
priests were all Syrian and Persian, and they spoke the Syrian
language in worship. In Mongol, Nestorian was deemed to be
the religion of the Kerite and the Ongut people. Stephen Neill
also expressed the same idea as follows: "But it is permissible to
wonder to what extent they really make their presence felt, and
how far their influence extended beyond the monastery walls.
Their task was entirely different from that of their fellow monks
in the wastes and forests of Central Europe."[25] If we put it in a
modern missionary term, Nestorian failed to practice "presence
theology" in Asia through which they should have demonstrated
the excellence of the Christian truth in their words and life.
Esther and Mordecai have become a great model of practiced

presence theology in Persia. Their wonderful presence in Persia attracted many Gentiles to the Jews: "And many people of other nationalities became Jews because fear of the Jews had seized them." (Esther 8: 17).   Finally, church division was an important factor of the disappearance of the Churches. This is still a serious problem in the churches of Asia. The deadliest obstacle to the Christian churches is to be found not outside it but within it. Unfortunately, it had happened in the Persian churches in the fourth century that the seminary school of Nisibis in Persia was destroyed not by Zoroastrian priests, but by dissension in its own Christian faculty.

In China, Nestorianism was misunderstood as a foreign religion, because the clergy was mostly Syrian and the language of worship was Syrian. This was the same in India where the people considered Nestorianism to be the religion of Persia. In addition to this, Nestorian Christians formed their own racial ghettoes of Syrians and Persians. They were hesitant to train and ordain the native leaders as pastors. It showed that they did not prepare the transfer of the mission work and property to the native church and national workers. The Syrian churches and Nestorians developed the monastery system. However, we do not read any story of revivals, reformation and evangelistic movements in their mission history. Many Nestorian monks and laypersons practiced devotion and commitment to God in communal life in the monastery. It is a separation model of devotion. They were not concerned about social and cultural transformation in the nation where they ministered. They formed their own a ghetto and stayed in isolation; consequently, they could not have fellowship with their neighbors. Nestorianism did not translate the Bible into native languages, so native believers could not read the Bible in their own language. In the early nineteenth century, the Church

Missionary Society (CMS) in India gathered information about the Thomas Syrian Church in 1818 and reported as follows:

> The present state of the Syrian Church is very low. It appears to have the form of Christianity, but little of the power... Ministers had no copies of the scriptures, but such Syriac Copies as were in the Public Service; and no book, except his Prayer-book, for his private use. Even Minister of the Churches have not a page of the scriptures for private study and devotion. The people have but little ideas of doing anything for support of their Ministers... Here are Churches built, and many of them fine noble structures-Christian Bishops and Ministers, with the Syriac scriptures in their hands, who needs only to be roused from their present lethargy state.[26]

We believe that the failure of the early Christianity in Asia needs to be examined from the point of theology: Many church historians agree that the apostolic Christian faith and doctrines were never preached and taught in Asia. From its inception, Nestorianism and other Christian groups who hold only one nature of Jesus Christ dominated the Churches in Persia and Arabia. Some theologians and western scholars ascribe the emergence of Muhamad to theology and church division in the Arabian Churches. We cannot consent to this criticism; however, the Christian churches are obliged to preach and teach biblical Christian messages and theology. The corruption of clergies and priests are pointed out as an important factor for the failure, and Nestorianism did not set up for national clergy and leadership of their churches. The impacts of the Syrian and the Persian churches were so strong in Asia that Christianity was considered a foreign religion. Nestorianism was a monastery-oriented church; they were not concerned on social transformation. The Bible was not translated into native languages. Finally, we do not read records of revival meeting and movements, and systematic evangelistic movements or reform movements. We believe that Asian Christianity never learned that the reformed churches always have to be reformed

(*Reformata ecclesia semper reformanda*). Again, we conclude that early Asian Christianity failed in church renewal and reformation.

Endnotes

[1] Samuel Moffett, *A History of Christianity in Asia,* vol. 1. (New York: Harper, 1992), 507.

[2] Henri Tessier, "The African root of Latin Christianity," www.30giornit. it/articoli_id_3553_13htm.

[3] L. W. Brown, *The Indian Christians of St. Thomas: An Account of the Ancient Syrian Church of Malabar* (Cambridge: The University Press, 1956), 139.

[4] K.S. Latourette, *Introducing Buddhism* (New York: Friendship Press, 1956), 10.

[5] Stephen Neill, A *History of Christian Missions* (New York: Penguin Book, 1964), 96.

[6] Philip Short, *Pol Pot: The History of a Nightmare* (London: John Murray, 2004), 150.

[7] Jason A Edward, "Pol Pot's Little Red Rock," https//socialhistory:org/ news/articles/10993

[8] K. S. Latourette, *Introducing Buddhism* (New York: Friendship Press, 1956), 50.

[9] Karl Barth, *Church Dogmatics,* 1/2, trans. G. T. Tompson and Harold Knight, (Edinburgh: T&T Clark, 1980), 341.

[10] Williston Walker, *A History of the Christian Church* (New York: Charles Scribner's Son, 1959), 57.

[11] Edward Gibbon, *The Decline and Fall of the Roman Empire* (Hertfordshire: Wordsworth, 1998), 252.

[12] Williston Walker, 58-59.

[13] The Syriac Orthodox Church," https://en.wikipedia.org/wiki/Syriac_ Orthodx_Church.

[14] F. Crawford Burkitt, *Early Eastern Christianity* (London: Gorgias Press, 2004), 90.

[15] F. Crawford Burkitt, 104.

[16] Crawford Burkitt, 108.

[17] John C. England, *The Hidden History of Christianity in Asia* (Delhi: ISPCK, 1996), 23.

[18] Paul Pierson, "Nestorian Mission," in *Evangelical Dictionary of World Missions* (Grand Rapids: Baker, 2000), 675.

[19] Paul Pierson, 675.

[20] John Steward, *The Story of a Church on Fire* (Edinburgh: T &T Clark, 1928), 90.

[21] John Steward, 91.

[22] Edward Gibbon, 797.

[23] Samuel Moffett, 507.

[24] Samuel Moffett, 505.

[25] Stephen Neill, 96.

[26] Church Missionary Society, *The Missionary Register for M DCCC XVIII* (London: L. B. Seeley, 1818), 110.

Chapter - 3

Reformation and Mission

The modern evangelical mission movements are the products of the Reformation. Nevertheless, many evangelical missiologists have raised serious questions as to the Reformer's missionary ideas. They argue that the Reformers such as Martin Luther, John Calvin, and Zwingli had no mission idea in their theology and ministry. As early as the late nineteenth century Gustav Warneck, the first evangelical missiologist in Germany, claimed for the first time that the Reformers had no conscious of mission theology and mission activities. Warneck's mission theory made a great impact on modern evangelical missions. He negatively comments on the Reformation as follows: "The comprehension of a continuous missionary duty of the Church was limited among the Reformers and their successors by narrow-minded dogmatism combined with a lack of historical sense. They knew of the great missions of the past, but according to their ideas the apostles had already gone forth to the whole world and they and their disciples had essentially accomplished the missionary task. Christianity, therefore, had already proved its universal vocation as a world religion."[1] K. S. Latourette accepted Warneck 's theoretical framework, and expressed a similar idea on the Reformation mission: "In contrast, by abandoning monasticism Protestants had deprived themselves of that instrument and most of their princes were so intent upon gaining the control of the Church in their domains by promoting Protestantism and were so engrossed in the struggle which engaged in its early years that they could give little attention to missions, even had they desired to do so. Some of the Protestant reformers were frankly no interested in missions to the non-Christians."[2]

In the early 20th century, the mission union movement and mission theories were begun to be developed; the Edinburgh Mission Conference in 1910 eventually evolved to the WCC in 1948. The liberal theology such as pluralism theology and the Social Gospel of Rauschenbush made a great impact on the evangelical missions at that time. Many people raised a question, "What is mission? Evangelism or Social Gospel?" The Renaissance and the Enlightenment philosophy have been more favored among the Christian churches and theologians than the Reformation faith and theology. So, Dr. Arthur Pierson (1837-1911), who was an American Presbyterian pastor, Christian leader, and mission leader, regarded liberalism as thee crisis of mission in his book *The Crisis of Missions* (1886). The concept of mission was so confused that Warneck wrote three volumes of the Evangelical Mission Theory (*Evangelische Missionslehere*, 1897, 1900, and 1902). Unfortunately, these books were not translated into English. Dr. Pierson and some evangelical missionary leader wrote the mission theories from the biblical perspectives.

It is to be noted that William Carey has sparked the assumption that the Reformers had not missionary ideas and theology. His book *An Enquiry into the Obligation of Christians to Use Means for the Conversion of the Heathens* (An Enquiry) is almost an epoch-making book in which he explicitly criticized the supposedly reason for the lack of the missionary ideas on the part of the

Reformers. However, Warneck's assumption has been countered by the same Lutheran theologians: Karl Sell,'s "Der Ursprung der urchristlichen und der modernen Mission," (the Rise of the early Christian and modern mission) *Zeitschrift fur Theologie und Kirche* (1895), W. Knopp, "Characteristerisches am Missionmotive der Englander," (Characteristics and motive of England Mission) *Allgemeine Missionseitschrift* 40 (1913), Hans Werner Gensichen's *Missionsgeschichte der neweren Zeit (Mission History of the New Era)* are representative theologians who developed the Reformation mission theology.

Assumption that the Reformation has no Mission

Warneck notes very well numerous reasons for the Reformers' absence of missionary thought. We summarize it: 1) The Reformers were preoccupied with the internal reform of the church; their manic concern to recover the Biblical Christianity from the Roman Catholic (the RC). The restoration of true doctrine and practice was their priority.

2) Reformers were almost crushed by external conflict with the Catholic princes: militarily and politically they were on the defensive and had no resources left for outreach. Their capacity was so limited that they could not think mission. 3) They were preoccupied with the heresy: The Pope and the Turk being apocalyptic figures, the two forms of antichrist, the shadow of their rebellion was cast over the peoples they dominate, which were all the near neighbors of the Protestant countries. One does not expect the conversion of antichrist. 4) They thought that the last day is at hand. This is Warneck's interpretation. We need more explanation about that. 5) The Reformers thought that the Great Commission was only given to the Apostles and they discharged it; the church is already everywhere. Today it is known that the

faculties of Wittenberg University had rejected the universal validity of spreading the Gospel when they were asked about it. 6) The Germans had no direct contact with heathen peoples; they had no non-Christian neighbors. The Reformers and subsequently the Protestants gave their priority to the Catholic Christians as the main target of evangelism and mission. A Lurtheran King of Denmark sent their missionaries to the northern part of Norway to convert the Catholic Christians to the Protestant Church.[3]

Latourette takes over Warneck's explanations and adds a few more by saying that social power was in the hands of princes who did not care for missions as much as Roman Catholic princes did. The Protestant nations' budding colonial interests were in the hands of trading companies who considered missionary concerns a waste of resources or even a threat to their income. The Protestants had no monks, having downgraded, for theological reasons, the idea of special religious vocation. Besides the reasons mentioned above, the concept of the church and the theology of the Reformation were also indicated for having weakened mission. Many people thought that the Reformation's definition of the church, as found in the sixteenth century confessions and catechisms, no longer served adequately to express what the church was. Nor did these confessional statements define what the task of the Church is in terms of God's purpose in its establishment. The critics argue that the doctrine of election did not allow room for human's efforts in missionary work. An example of this was expressed well in the conversation of William Carey with a Calvinist preacher when Carey intended to go to India as a missionary. It is told that the Calvinist preacher said to Carey, "if God willed the conversion of heathen, he could do it without your help."

The doctrine of eschatology is also pointed out as one of the important reasons: The critics claimed that the Reformers believed that people of other faiths had already been reached by the Gospel and were condemned by God due to their rejection of the message of salvation. The German missiologist Julius Richter contends that the Reformer's eschatology or millennialism crippled the Church's missionary activities rather than incited them. Luther expected the last days to come sometime in the year 1558.[4] The Lutheran theologian Philip Nicolai expected the Parousia (the end of time) to take place around year 1670. It indicates that some Lutheran theologians seem to be pessimistic on the human history.

Finally, the Reformer's denial of mission society is the most important reason for the destitute of mission in the Reformation theology. It is true that the Reformers were averse to the monastery orders of the RC. For the RC the mission works have become the primary duty of the monastery orders, the Catholic churches did not involve in mission. Ralph Winter an American missiologist from whom I learned the mission history in Fuller Seminary during the 1970s highly praised the monastery orders of the RC, saying that the religious orders provided the RC with spiritual vitality and missions. Winter proposed the two structures of God's redemptive mission for the world mission: the sodality and the modality structure. Some missiologists express the sodality as a para-church organization. For Ralph Winter, the denomination churches belong to the modality and the interdenominational mission society is the sodality. He argues that "the harmony between the modality and the sodality achieved by the Roman Church is perhaps the most significant characteristics of this phase of the world Christian movement."[5] He supported the sodality structure than the modality for missions, so he did not agree with the Reformer's view on the monastery orders. He said that "Protestant knowing about monasteries may be correct for certain situations, but the popular Protestant stereotype surely cannot describe correctly all that happened during the 1000 years! ...and any generalization about so vast a phenomenon is bound to be simply an unreliable and no doubt prejudice caricature."[6] However, it is our regret that Ralph do not see the monastery orders from the Biblical principle and moral dimension, he positively evaluate it only from mission perspectives. Unfortunately, Winter missed seeing the negative sides of the Jesuits missions in the mission history at all.

Reply to the Criticism:

Reformation restored Biblical Christianity

The criticisms that the Reformation has no missionary idea and theology shows some serious faults: Many Calvinist theologians have defended that the Reformation was itself a missionary movement on a grand and international scale. First, the critics solely dismissed that the 5 sola of the Reformation are the core messages of evangelism and mission. The 5 sola are solus Christus (only Christ), sola fide (only faith), sola gratia (only grace), sola scriptura (only Bible), *sola Deo gloria* (glory only to God). Again, the Reformers recovered the true Christianity from the RC. The Catholic placed the authority of their institutionalized Church above the authority of the Bible and has monopolized Christianity for one thousand years in the name of Christendom by excluding and severely persecuting the other Christian churches. From the beginning the Catholic absolutely rejected the emergences of diverse Christian churches besides the Catholic. A Lutheran theologian Karl Holsten maintains that Luther's concept of the Church and the words of God had made the Church's mission possible. Luther's concept of mission is the gathering of the elect, the people of God out of the nations.[7] Many Christians misunderstand that the evangelical Christianity came from the

England Methodist John Wesley. They do not know who coined the term "evangelical" in the church history for the first time. It is Luther who challenged the supremacy of institutional church above the authority of the Bible. He claimed that the "evangel" (evangelism) of the Bible is the first, next the Church comes out. The theology of the Reformation is that the Bible created Christian church: it is not the Church that has made the Bible. With respect to this, Luther is a founder of evangelical Church. A close friend of Luther once asked him , "The churches started by you would be called the Lutheran Church?" Luther replied, "No, it would be called the Evangelical Churches." Now in Germany the *Evangelischen Kirchen* (evangelical Churches) denotes Protestant Churches, not evangelical churches what we perceive in the English-speaking world.

Reformers and Salvation Experience

Those who have experienced regeneration have a spiritual desire to share the blessings of salvation with his or her neighbors. Who can say that the Reformers did not have that idea? The Reformers confessed that they have had a salvation experience through spiritual and theological conflicts. For Luther, believer's personal experience of the saving grace of God necessarily brings the preaching of the Gospel to other people. Luther sums it all up in the famous metaphor of the stone thrown into water: it produces circular waves which moves out from the center in successive progression; in the same way the Word of God moves out into the world, beginning from Jerusalem to the ends of the earth.

The mission history demonstrated that the Lutheran churches and the Calvinist churches had actively engaged in the foreign mission. The offsprings of the Reformation have experience the love of God, so they were eager to share God's blessings with the neighbor as well as the people in the gentile world. The critics of the Reformation much focused on that the Reformer confined the great commission, "Go and make disciples of all nations" (Matt. 28:19) to only the Apostles. In this issue we need to consider that the Reformers denied the apostolic successor of the Pope, accordingly, they emphasized the cessation of the Apostolic office as an extra-office of the Church. The Reformers interpreted that the cessation of the Apostle office inevitably extended to the missionary commandment. The Faculty of Wittenberg University had rejected the universal validity of the mission works.

However, we need to notice that the great commission did not work as sole motive of mission works in the mission history. Van den Berg a Dutch missiologist explained in his excellent dissertation *Constrained by the Love of Christ* suggested that the love of God was the striking motive for the foreign missions in England and in the U. S.: "For Christ's love compels us, because we are convinced that one died for all; and therefore all died." (2 Cor.5:14). The revival movements and the Great Awakening sparked the missionary movements in England and America in the eighteenth and nineteenth century. A German missiologist W. Knopp made a very interesting comparison between England and Germany in terms of their missionary forces in the early twentieth century. In the late nineteenth and early twentieth century the German churches had sent about only 900 missionaries and England about 2,700 missionaries respectively overseas. Knopp ascribe the reason for the fewer missionaries from the German Churches than from England to the weaker conviction of the Scriptures as the Word of God in the German churches because they were influenced by liberal theology.[8]

Theology and Mission of the Reformation

The Reformation provided the Churches with mission theology and messages. Luther's "justification by faith" is the core of missionary message. John Calvin's theology is practical, ministry-oriented, and concerned with society, and his Biblical theology essentially is practical and missionary. Calvin was a great evangelist and Christian educator: Through the Geneva Academy he established the evangelization of Europe many reformers who spread to bring the Gospel to their nation. This achievement came through his synthesis of theology and evangelism. Calvinism is an excellent example of good balance between theology and evangelism. John Knox is a brilliant Presbyterian who learned from Calvin and introduced democratic system of Presbyterianism to Scotland. We need to acknowledge that Calvin's time is entirely different from the twenty-first century in which we are living. But he was not blind or deaf to the heathen world and its need. Calvin's knowledge of the pagan nations was taken from the Bible and literatures. He also considered the threat of the Ottoman Turks seriously and mentioned the Turks 4 times in his *Institutes of Christian Religion (Institutes)*. The Turks denotes the Muslims.

Calvin emphasized the mission to the Gentile world. He said that the Lord Jesus Christ did not come to reconcile a few individuals only to God the Father but to extend his grace over all the world (Sermon on I Tim. 225, cf. Commentary Isaiah 124 Mich. 43).[9] Luther emphasizes that magistrate had a special duty to spread Christianity in their lands. That idea is much like the doctrine of *cuius regio eius religio* that figured so prominently in the Roman Catholic. We suppose that from this idea later the Lutheran Churches had become state church in the Northern Europe including Germany. On the other hand, the Calvinist churches of the Presbyterian and the Reformed churches insisted on the separation between government and church.

The critics of the Reformation stress that the doctrine of the election and eschatology served to weaken mission. It comes from the ignorance of the mission history. The mission history tells us that the doctrine of eschatology and election rather helped to strengthen missions: Hans E. Gensichen argues that Luther's eschatology did not prevent him from vigorously promoting mission. Apocalyptic expectations thus do not necessarily paralyze missionary efforts.[10] Even more significant is the fact that Luther's contemporaries, the Anabaptists, adhered to eschatological views not essentially different from his, yet in their case precisely these views inspired them to missionary involvement. Many Presbyterian denominations in the U.S. and Korea firmly holding to the election doctrine have become a majority in the world mission. For Calvin the doctrine of election does not exclude mission and evangelism. The hyper-Calvinism denies the missionary duty of the Church to the world, arguing that the responsibility to save the heathen people totally belongs to God. But the doctrine of election also needs an instrument through which man can come to know Jesus Christ as Savior. Calvin demonstrated in his *Institutes* (Book 3, 23:12-14) that the doctrine of predestination does not contradict evangelism and missions. Not only did he defend the doctrine of predestination, but also calls for the church to do evangelism by saying that: "because we know not who belongs to the number of the predestinated or who does not belong, our desire ought to be that all may be saved; and hence every person we meet, we will desire to be with us a partaker of our peace." (Inst. III, 23:14).

The Reformers' doctrine of eschatology did not hinder missions. This view also theologically and dogmatically misconstrues the Reformation Churches' theology. The mission history tells us that their eschatology stimulated the missionary work of the churches. The eschatological vision impelled some Puritans to a vital concern for the conversion of their countrymen and the Indians, and it is well known that one of the nineteenth century's missionary motives was the doctrine of eschatology. Hudson Taylor and many young missionaries were motivated by the second coming of Jesus to go to the mission fields.

Eschatology and Mission

Most critics of the Reformation mission misunderstand that the doctrine of eschatology hinders mission motive. This is a misunderstanding of the Reformer's eschatology. David Bosch argues that "Calvin subscribed to an eschatology in the process of being fulfilled. He used the term *regnum Christi* (the reign of Chris) in this respect, viewing the church as intermediary between the exalted Christ and the secular order. Such a theological departure could not but give rise to the idea of mission as extending the reign of Christ, both by the inward spiritual renewal of individuals and by transforming the face of the earth filling with the knowledge of the Lord."[11] In the 18th century, the doctrine of eschatology began to be seriously discussed in the American churches; the millennialism is deeply related to the eschatology. At that time many American Christians thought that the eve of the millennium had come, and that Christ might soon be expected to come in glory. After the Great Awakening, millennial expectation became the common property of virtually in all American Protestants.[12] There was an intimate relation between mission and millennium expectation. The thought of imminent advent of the millennium made a great impact on the mission movements in the American churches. It is to be noticed that the millennium expectation had been strong among the Presbyterian churches.

Luther and the Jews

We want to give our attention to Luther's ethno-theology on the Jews and the Turks (Muslims). At the time of the Reformation the Jews and Muslims had become an important issue in Western Christianity. The anti-Semitism had been sweeping over Europe, and Muslims were considered Satanic. That was the same with the Reformers. In 1546 the Byzantine Empire of the Greek Orthodox Church was conquered by the Ottoman Turks of Islam. Luther preached it as God's judgment on the corrupted Greek Orthodox Church. Luther was deeply concerned about Islam in Turkey, so his writings have been subjects of special studies by many German missiologists, and Luther's view of the Jews seems to still remain controversial, whether Luther showed his feeling of hate against them or not. "Luther calls the Jews the worst enemies of the church. However, these statements are more gentile than in his later works."[13]

Luther had made a harsh proposal that "Jews' traveling in Germany should be limited, or they should even be driven away from Germany to their own country."[14] Despite his negative views on the Jews, he had a vision of winning them to Christian faith. In Wikipedia an unknown scholar states : "However, despite his importance as a figure in the development of Protestant theology, his positions on Judaism continue to be controversial. These changed dramatically from his early career, where he showed concern for the plight of European Jews to his later years, when embittered by his failure to convert them to Christianity, he became outspokenly anti-Semitic in his statements and writings. Recent historical studies have focused on Luther's influence on modern antisemitism, with a particular focus on Adolf Hitler and the Nazis."[15]

Not Mission Society, But the Church!

With respect to the monastic orders of the RC, the Reformers'
main concern largely have focused on the recovery of true doctrine
and moral purity of the church. They were disapproval of the
monastic orders whose reputation was negatively known among
the Christian churches in the medieval age. The Reformers do
not view the ascetic monk as biblical. Luther saw fundamental
flaw in monasticism that it is only an escape from the world.
He wrote "For we are not made for fleeing human company but
for living in society and sharing good and evil." Luther called
for the abolition of monasteries and return of monks and nuns
to secular life. He repudiated monastic worship as blasphemous
and wasted efforts.

However, Calvin did not exclude in his theological discussion
monasticism at all. In his *Institutes* 4:13, 21, he positively mentions
the monastery of the early Churches by quoting the words of
Augustine: the most saint comes from the monastery, at the same
time the most evil-man comes from the monastery. He was a fierce
critic of the monasteries of the medieval churches. He regarded
monasticism as schismatic of the church (*Institutes*, 4: 13, 14).
"Do they not separate from the legitimate society of the faithful,
by acquiring for special ministry and private administration of the
sacrament?"[16] Calvin was convinced that mission is the church's
obligation. The reason is that the treasure of the Gospel is deposited
in the Church, so the Church should be the subject of mission.
Following this principle, the Calvinistic churches organized the
mission societies for the foreign missions.

The Missions after the Reformation

The Reformation churches needed to take a long time to settle
down and expand their reform movements in their nation, however,

they launched the mission works to the end of the earth. The Protestant churches rapidly expanded in Europe; the Protestant churches began to spread in the nations of England, Scotland, Holland, and France. The modern churches who have no concerns on the confession and basic Christian doctrines need to notice that the Reformers gave their emphasis to the confession of faith and the catechism. Laying doctrinal and theological foundation, they immediately launched missionary undertakings. William Brown made a meaningful comment on the early Reformation missions: "At the Reformation the light of the gospel burst forth on the nations of Europe, like the sun in the morning after a dark night. By degrees, it spread from country to country and dispelled the shades of ignorance and error, in which they had been enveloped for a series of ages."[17] The important characteristics of the Reformation missions can be summarized as follows:

First, their missions have been thoroughly Church centered mission, not inter-denominational mission society (sodality structure). They made mission organization only within their churches. The nineteenth denomination mission society of the Presbyterian churches in America rests on the Reformation mission. The Puritans founded the Society for the Propagation of the Gospel in New England for the Indian missions in which John Elliot's influences was great. It was the first Protestant mission society exclusively devoted to missions. This Society sent John Elliot, David Brainerd, David Zeisberger, and Marcus Whitman to the American Indians.

Second, the Reformation missions much rested on the immigrations. The Puritans in England immigrated to North America in order to escape from the persecution of the Church of England; the French Protestants the Huguenotes (Calvinist Protestants) immigrated to South Africa and some to Latin

America. The Huguenotes rapidly multiplied during the persecution by the Catholic King. Calvin's influences increased in France and French Protestants. In 1555 there was a congregation in Paris, but 1559 they organized the First General Synod in Paris and adopted a strong Calvinistic creed and the Presbyterian constitution drawn from Calvin's ecclesiastical principles.[18] Those who developed the watch industry in Switzerland were the Huguenotes who immigrated from France.

Third, the first mission project of the Lutheran mission collaborated with the Danish crown. Later the Lutheran Churches became the state-church. In 1559, Gustavus Vasa, King of Sweden, sent a missionary to the Lapland with the view of extending Christianity among the inhabitants of that country; the people "were still sunk in all the horrors of Pagan ignorance and superstition."[19] The Lutheran mission could be undertaken where Lutheran authorities ruled.

Fourth, the Reformation missions endeavored to translate the Bible, the Confessions, and the Catechism which could strengthen the basic Christian faith and doctrines. And they were not slow to set up (ordain or appoint) the native minister which have been much neglected in the Nestorian and the Catholic missions. From the inception of their mission works, they realized the value of a qualified, committed native worker in the mission fields. They followed Paul's model that Paul appointed the elders in the Church of Ephesus after about 3 years of mission and ministry.

Fifth, the Reformation missions from the outset made the Catholic Christians their mission target. Luther and Calvin were too negative to the Catholics and the Pope and this might have greatly impacted the Protestant missions, it was evidenced that many Reformed theologians and pastors would evaluate the mission works of the Catholic very negatively. Even in the early nineteenth century the Protestants mission leaders saw the Catholic as superstition. William Brown's following sentences reflect this: "Fired with a sacred zeal for the cause of religion, the reformers followed superstition to her most secret haunts, brought her forth to the view of the world, and exposed her in al her native deformity."[20] In India, the Lutheran missionaries converted many Catholic Christians to the Lutheran Churches, so there were numerous clashes between the Lutheran missionaries and the Catholic missionaries.

Lutheran missions

In the year 1559, the celebrated Gustavus Vasa, King of Sweden, sent a missionary to the Lapland with the view of extending Christianity among the inhabitants of that country; the people "were still sunk in all the horrors of Pagan ignorance and superstition." In Brown's writings we read much about the term "superstition" which denotes the Catholic. German Pietism produced the Halle-Daish missions from 1705 onward in which the Zinzendorf's Herrnhurt played a leading role in the Lutheran mission. "Soon after the commencement of the eighteenth century, Frederick the Fourth, king of Denmark involved in sending the Lutheran missionaries for the conversion of the heathen on the cost of the East Indies. Bartholome Ziegenbalg and Henry Plutcho were embarked at Copenhagen in 1705 and arrived in July 1706 at Tranquebar in the East India.

Presbyterian (Puritans) Missions

Most people do not know that that Calvin and the Swiss church sent five missionaries to Brazil with a Huguenot navy admiral, Nicolas Durand de Villegagnon. Calvin and the newly planted few churches in Switzerland planned and organized a foreign mission enterprise. William Brown lists the fourteen missionaries who were sent to Brazil from Geneva in 1556. He describes it as follows: "Engaged in propagating the light of the gospel through the benighted kingdom of Christendom, the reformers could scarcely be expected to direct their attention to the heathen world. But notwithstanding the magnitude of their other exertions, this object was not entirely overlooked by them. In 1556, fourteen Protestant missionaries, namely, Philip Corgviller, Peter Richer, William Charters, Peter Bordonne, Matthew Verneville John Bordele, Andrew Font, Nicolas Dyonysius, John Gardienne, Martin David, Nicolas Ravequet, James Rufus, Nicolas Carmille, and John James Levius, were sent by the church of Geneva to plant the Christian faith in the lately discovered regions of America.[21] Unfortunately, the French Admiral Villegagnon abandoned the Reformed faith to return to the Catholic and the Catholic churches severely persecuted them; some of them returned to Swiss and some have been killed and persuaded by the Catholic.

Calvinism made a great impact on the Netherlands; many theologians applied Calvin's *soli Deo gloria* and *regnum Christi* to mission theory: the representative theologians are Hadrianus Saravia (1531-1613), Gisbertus Voetius (1588-1676), Jestus Hernhuis (1589-1676), Voetius suggested the objects of mission as the glory of God, the conversion of heathen and the church planting, and J. Hernhuis, as early as the seventeenth century, warned of the danger of the British colonialism in India in his book *De lagatione evangelica ad Indos capessenda admonitio* (Evangelical mission to India and its Warnings 1618). His warning came out in 18 years after the East India Company was started. He was a missionary to India, pastor, and theologian. The Dutch reformed churches made their spread in Sri Lanka, Indonesia, South Africa through colonialism.

In 1658 the Netherlands defeated the Portuguese and they occupied Sri Lanka. Sadly, the Protestant nation the Netherlands also repeated forced conversion as the Catholic nations did. The Netherlands colonial government issued a proclamation that only natives converted from Catholic or Buddhism to Dutch Reformed Church can be employed to public office; the converted natives subscribed the Helvetic Confession of the Faith and professed himself a member of the Reformed church. This absurd and impolite order was so well calculated to make the people hypocrites, not Christians. The Dutch Reformed Churches planted many churches in Sri Lanka and later the native churches grew to form the Christian Reformed Church in Sri Lanka. However, in Indonesia some colonial government offices prohibited their missionary from doing mission to the Muslims. At present Indonesia remains the largest Muslim nation, while Sri Lanka is a militant Buddhism nation.

The Reformed churches and the Presbyterian churches shared the same Calvinism with a little difference of church government, but the Presbyterian churches have engaged more active missions than the Reformed churches. It has been evidenced in Korea: Mr. Horae Allen is the first Presbyterian missionary to Korea (1885), in fact, he was an ordained minister of the Reformed Church of America (RCA) graduated in the Reformed seminary. With a fervent zeal for mission, he applied to the Mission Board of the RCA for going to Korea as a missionary. But his proposal was turned down for financial reasons. The American Northern Presbyterian mission accepted him and sent him to the hermit nation Korea where mission was prohibited. Since he came to Korea he was known as a Presbyterian man. In 2002 a leader of the RCA visited the Korean churches, and he publicly confessed in a meeting with the Korean church leaders that the RCA still regrets it.

Moravian Mission

We thought that all the Protestant Churches come from the Reformation of Luther and Calvin; for in Korea and the South Asia there are not Moravian churches. The original name *Unitas Fratrum* (the Unity of Brethren) is called the Moravians, the United Brethren or the Moravian Church. The Moravians go back its history to John Hus who suffered martyrdom in 1416. He was 100 years ahead of Luther. The Moravian Church is a good model of the combination of Church and mission, for them the church itself is mission, there is no dichotomy between the church and mission. The Moravian missions should be examined with the Count Zinzendorf of the Herrnhut in Moravia. From the Herrnhut many Moravian missionaries were sent to many nations: "In the short period of eight or nine years, they sent missionaries to Greenland, to St. Thomas, to St. Crois, to Surinam, to the Rio de Berbice, to the Indians of North America, to the Negroes of South Carolina, to Lapland, to Tartry, to Algiers, to Guinea, to the Cape of Good Hope, and to the island of Ceylon."[22] A Korean professor Dr. Ryoo summarized the Moravians mission strategies as 1) Christ-centered messages, 2) Dependency on the Holy Spirit, 3) Fervent prayer, 4) Pietism, 5) Contextualization, 6) Tentmaking, 7) Layperson missionary, and commitment to mission.[23] Within twenty years of their commencement of their mission works, the Moravian Brethren sent more missionaries than Anglicans and the other Protestants during the two preceding centuries. They established mission strategy on which they would carry their mission works in mission fields. The Moravian mission became a good model of tent-making by studying medicine, geography, and language, and other necessary skills for self-support. The Moravian missions influenced John Wesley and William Carey.

Many evangelical missiologists have argued that the Reformers did not engage in missionary work due to circumstantial and doctrinal reasons or their wrong interpretation of the Great Commission. But the alleged lack of missionary work with the Reformers should not be attributed to these factors. Rather it must be ascribed to their successors. Many confessed Calvinists have not a spark of Calvin's zeal for the Gospel. An unfortunate dichotomy between theology and mission is seen today in many Churches. There is a tendency, on the one hand, for missions to sacrifice theology, while, on the other hand, the theology-oriented churches have no concern for missions. Reformers such as Luther and Calvin attempted to maintain a balance between theology and mission. We need to maintain the same balance. The vigorous missionary movement of the Presbyterian Church in America and Korea demonstrates that the Reformed Church is a missionary church. The mission organization that sent the most missionaries in Korea are the denomination mission boards of many Presbyterian Churches.

Endnotes

[1] Gustav Warneck, *Outline of a History of Protestant Missions from the Reformation to the Present Time* (New York: Revell, 1902), 90.

[2] K. S. Latourette, *A History of Christianity,* Vol. 2 (New York: Harper& Row Brothers, 1970), 96.

[3] John Yoder, "Reformation and Mission: Literature Review," *Occasional Mission Bulletin Journal* 22 (1971): 1-2.,"

[4] Julius Richter, *Evangelisches Missionskunde* (Leipzig: Dieterchterische, 1927), 2-3.

[5] Ralph Winter, "The Two Structures of God's Redemptive Mission," ww.w.undertheiceberg.com/wp..content/uproad2006/4.

[6] Ralph Winter, "The Two Structures of God's Redemptive Mission,"

[7] Von Walter Holsten, "Reformation und Mission," *ArchyfürReformartionsgeschichte 44* (1953):9.

[8] W. Knopp, "Charakteristerisches am Missionmotive der Englander," *Allgemeine Missionzeitschrift* 40: (1913): 563-64.

[9] Thomas Torrance, *Kingdom and Church* (London: Essential Book, 196), 161.

[10] Hans W. Gensichen, "Were the Reformers Indifferent to Missions?" in *History's Lessons for Tomorrow's Mission* (Geneva: WSCF, 1960): 122.

[11] David Bosch, *Transforming Mission: Paradigm Shifts in Theology of Mission* (Maryknoll: Orbis Books, 2008), 256.

[12] David Bosch, 314.

[13] Pekka Huhtinen, Luther and World Missions: A Review," *Concording Theological Quarterly* 65:1 (January 2001): 24.,

[14] Pekka Huhtinen, 27.

[15] Martin Luther "https://en.wikipedia.org/wiki/Martin_Luther_and_anti_semitism.

[16] Luther and Calvin https//heidelblog.net/2014/03/did-luther-calvin-favor-evangelical-monsticism.

[17] William Brown, 18.

[18] Williston Walker, 381.

[19] William Brown, 20

[20] William Brown, 17.

[21] William Brown, 17.

[22] William Brown, 289.

[23] David Eung-Yul Ryoo, The Moravian Mission Strategy: Christ-Centered, Mission-Minded," *Haddington House Journal* 2008: 35-49.

Chapter - 4

Nineteenth Century Mission History

Nineteenth century missions were the result of the Great Awakening and other revival movements in Anglo-Saxon nations. Almost without exception, the missionaries of the nineteenth century were men and women of compassion with a deep conviction and desire to save perishing souls from perdition. They believed that the heathen were lost without the knowledge of Jesus Christ. They spared no pain to take the gospel to the lost and dying before it was too late. Pearl Buck, in the biography of her parents, described nineteenth century missionaries as follows: "The early missionaries were born warriors and very great men, for in those days religion was still a banner under which to fight. No weak or timid soul could sail the seas to foreign lands and defy death and danger unless he did carry religion as his banner; under which even death itself would be a glorious end. To go forth, to cry out, to save others, these were frightful urgencies upon the soul already saved. There was a very madness of necessity – an agony of salvation."[1]

However, there was a shift of mission motives from doing missions purely for the glory of God to doing missions to convert the heathen in the evangelical mission movement. The major motive in American missions from the seventeenth century until the late eighteenth century was for the glory of God. "For the Puritans, the ultimate goal of mission remained, as it did for Voetius, the glory of God, which R. P. Beaver calls the taproot of mission of the church. It was undoubtedly a potent motive for missionary involvement in the two centuries of Protestant mission." [2] But most strangely, this motive lost influence and was replaced by motives of obedience to Christ and a pity for the perishing souls of the heathen. It demands notice that Paul's ministry was a ministry of glory and the doxological mode in missions goes beyond optimism in the expectation of response.

Despite the sacrifices of many missionaries and investments of financial resource, regrettably evangelical missions have failed in Asia. Some Asian Christian leaders largely ascribe it to incorrect mission strategy and western colonialism. The emergence of the ecumenical movements in the twentieth century greatly challenged the evangelical missions in their concept of mission. This chapter attempts to defend the evangelical concept of the missions and briefly introduce the criticisms of ecumenical theologians. Above all, we are working in Southeast Asia, so we briefly mention the churches and institutions established by independent missions and denomination missions.

Evangelization Priority Mission

The main features of the 19th century missions can be summarized as follows. First, the revival movements of the nineteenth century created many mission societies in the West including the American Board of Commissioners for Foreign Missions (ABCFM), 1810, the American Baptist Missionary Union, 1814, the board of the Reformed Dutch Church, 1832, the Presbyterian Board of the Foreign Missions, 1833, the Protestant Episcopal Board of

Missions, 1833, the Evangelical Lutheran Missionary Society 1844, and the Southern Presbyterian Board, 1861.

Second, missions and colonialism are associated with each other with the most mission work done in regions occupied or colonized by Western colonial powers. The East India Company helped build a bridge for missions, but sometimes they hindered it with their business affairs and national interests. Colonialism has led to Christianity being rejected by many of the nationals or the natives in mission fields.

Third, Christian missions instigated the clashes between Christianity and native cultures. Putting it in other words, it is a clash of value systems between individualistic Christian religion and collectivistic Asian religion. Christianity was not successful in Christianizing any nation of Asia. The Christian population in the Philippines accounts for 90%, but nobody considers the Philippines a Christian nation. Contrary to this, Islam conquered many of the Christian nations of the Middle East to make them Islamic nations. In South Asia, Islam successfully Islamized the Hindu-Buddhist Malaysia and Indonesia. The nineteenth century evangelical missions were very optimistic that Western civilization and Christian missions would transform the whole world. We need to notice that in the nineteenth century the enlightenment philosophy, communism and early Western cultural anthropology were dominated by the same optimism that non-Christian religions and culture would slowly weaken and eventually disappear on earth. The optimism has been proved futile; rather, we see the resurgence of other religions in Asia.

Fourth, Protestant missions gained more converts among the animistic tribal people or minority ethnic groups: Karen in Myanmar, Bataks and Kalimantans in Indonesia, and Naga tribes in northeast India. Except for the Karen, these ethnic groups were head-hunting groups, but they became Christians through group conversions or people movements.

Fifth, while the Western missionaries were bringing the Gospel to Asia, the West exported enlightenment philosophy, secular ideologies, and science to Asia; Asian intellectuals and the young generation welcomed them more than Christian truth. Secular philosophy, communism, evolution, nationalism, and science have captured the hearts of Asian intellectuals and the young generation. Communism has conquered many Asian countries without paying great sacrifices and costs.

Asia: Lands of Darkness

The Asian countries where Western missionaries set foot were characterized by the uncivilized and backward traditions of religion and superstition. India and China were very proud of their long history and great civilization. In our school systems we learned that China and India were the origins of ancient civilization

An American Reformed theologian Charles Hodge (1797-1878) evaluated India as follows:

> Long before Greece or Rome became cultivated communities, and when Europe was the home only of uncivilized barbarians, India was covered with rich and populous cities; the arts had reached highest state of development; a literature and language which, in the judgment of scholars, rival those of Greece and Rome, had been produced, and a system of philosophy as profound, as subtle and as diversified as the human mind ever elaborated, were already taught in her schools.[3]

Dr. Charles Hodge was a man of the middle of the nineteenth century; many Western missionaries arrived in India at that time, but there is a radical contrast between the view of Charles Hodge and the missionaries' rhetoric and writings about India. The missionaries negatively expressed the Indian culture and religions, referring to Hindus as Hindoos, Muslims as Mohammedans and Animism and Shamanism as superstition. Latourette listed the social evils in Asia and Africa: "Child marriage, the immolation of widows, temple prostitution, and untouchability in India; foot binding, opium addiction, and the abandoning of babies in China; polygamy, the slave trade and the destruction of twins in Africa."[4]

James Denis's *Christian Missions and Social Progress: A Sociological Study of Foreign Missions* describes how missions have contributed to civilization. James Dennis divided the non-Christian world into three categories: semi-civilized, barbarians, and savage people. This dividing is enough to provoke the people of non-Western world. He defines semi-civilized as designated races comparatively advanced in culture and representing in varying degrees some of the characteristics of the higher civilization. Of this class Japanese, Chinese, and in many respects Indian society would be an illustrative example.[5] The "barbarous" would denote a lower grade of social life, yet not so degraded and brutalized as to be ranked among savages; for example, Central Asia, Arabia and the coast line of Northern Africa would be classed as barbarous. Savage is the lowest grade of native society. He did not mention South East Asia and Korea.

Denis called India semi-civilized, but in India what William Carey observed and experienced was far from civilization. In 1799, William Carey happened to witness a horrible scene of Indian Sati burning the wife of the dead husband to death. He wrote a vivid impression in his diary as follows:

> Being evening, we got out of the boat to walk, when we saw a number of people assembled on the river-side. I asked them what they were met for, and they told me to burn the body of a dead

man. I inquired if his wife would die with him; they answered
Yes, and pointed to the woman. I asked if this was the woman's
choice, or if she were brought to it by any improper influences.
They answered that voluntarily. We could not bear to see more,
but left them, exclaiming loudly against the murder, full of horror
at what we had seen.[6]

When Adoniram Judson came to Myanmar in 1813, the U.S.
Baptist missionaries described Myanmar's political situation as
politics being a dictatorship, different from region to region, and
civil servants low, vicious and cruel. There was no civilization at
all. Fortunately, however, the king described himself as a merciful
man, intelligent and gentle. Most Asia nations were poor and
made up of a feudal society of rulers and subjects. Politically, it
was an undemocratic government of absolute authority, governed
by tribal chiefs and kings. The illiteracy rate was high and there
were no administration, education, hospitals and welfare systems.
However, religion and traditional culture exerted a strong binding
force on the society and politics. There were many tribal groups
of different languages and customs, but they did not have their
own alphabet and letters. The words such as rational thought and
scientific proof were unfamiliar terminology. The schools, hospitals,
and administrative and parliamentary systems that exist now are
the products of modernization and missionary works. For example,
in the 19th century, Korea was a poor and uncivilized society.
A Korean gentleman asked a Canadian missionary James Gale,
"In this world, is there a poorer country than Korea?" American
missionary William Blair came to Pusan to look around the city
and explained his impressions as follows: "Fusan (Pusan) is not
then worthy to be called city. It was just a collection of mud-
walled, straw-thatched huts with here and a tile-roofed house
among them, all so low that one could stand in the street and
put his hand on the roof of any one of them. It was hardly fair
to speak of streets at all."[7]

Civilization for Evangelism

Most missionaries who came to Asia wanted to share the salvation message with perishing souls in Asia, but most nations were closed to missions. Most missionaries did not intend to conduct civilization missions, but because of closed countries, civilization was only the way for them, so they opened schools, hospitals, clinics, medical colleges, orphanages, and leprosaria. Concerning this issue, a Japanese church leader properly commented that the American mission boards who sent their missionaries to Japan ordered their missionaries to give their priority to evangelism, but they could not do direct evangelism because of the socio-political situation of Japan. He summarizes the characteristics of the American missionaries as people who had personally experienced conversion, who believed the Bible as the inspired and infallible words of God, practiced a strict moral life, and had a strong zeal for evangelism with strong sense of the superiority of western civilization. Despite their strong zeal for evangelism they could not but change their mission strategy. However, they were reportedly a little frustrated with the response of the mission board, because the mission board wanted the fruits of the mission by numbers of conversion. We need to notice that when the missionaries retired to go back home, they were also not satisfied with small numbers of conversion.[8]

In the early nineteenth century most missionaries were involved in education. Alexander Duff is known as the model of education mission. He was sent by the Church of Scotland, and at that time the moderate party in the Church insisted on education missions. However, many missionaries were doubtful of this course. Nevertheless, Duff approached the question of education with energy, skill, and vision, which was rewarded with rapid and unprecedented success, the result being that the importance of education as missions in India was never seriously doubted again. The school founded by Duff developed to become the present-day Scottish Church College. It had a broad curriculum with everything from fundamental Christian teaching to scientific subjects. Duff regarded science as "the record and interpretation of God's invisible handwork." He saw "Hinduism as the root of India's problems, but he was hardly less implacably opposed to Western secularism."[9] He thought that if the Indian young men and women learn Christian religion, English and western science, they would be easier to convert to Christianity.[10] A missionary in India reports the significance of the school as follows: "Schools are arising in all quarters; natives volunteering, and anxiously seeking the establishment of them in their villages. The only limitation to their number results from the want of Funds; so that the invisible prejudices of the Natives, as they are called, are giving way." [11] Civilization has never succeeded in terms of conversion and church growth in mission history. However, it could become the point of contact with non-Christian community; the missionaries and national Christians could demonstrate their excellence in the integrity of character and morality through the service in institutions and schools.

Indigenous Churches and Indigenous Principles

In the middle of the nineteenth century, civilization mission began to be challenged by the nationalists as well as the self-support mission principles. The nationalists criticized civilization as westernization and secularization, while many mission leaders called for a return to the biblical principles of mission strategy. They argued that civilization mission also demands too much financial resources and it is not a genuine mission. Dr. Arthur Glasser denigrated civilization mission as "old paternalism and hand-out approach to the beggars".[12] In India civilization strategy has helped educate Indian intellectuals; these intellectuals have been employed in the important positions of the central and local government and it provoked the Hinduism leaders and the national leaders. To their eyes, Western missionaries were only the British colonialists who invaded India. The evangelical mission leaders believed that to regenerate the individual is the best way to civilization. Dennis reiterates the priority of evangelism over civilization as follows: "Civilization, it is acknowledged, is not the chief aim of mission; nor does the general betterment of society represent high motive. At the same time, we should gladly note amazing effects of the Christian religion, wherever accepted, in producing a nobler moral tone and a better social environment. A soul which is saved by the Gospel is redeemed for this world as well as for the next."[13]

The three-self formula of self-support, self-government, and self-propagation gives its priority to evangelism and church planting. Henry Venn, the general secretary of the Church Missionary Society (CMS), and Rufus Anderson, the general secretary of the ABCFM, proposed their ideas at almost the same time. Anderson and Venn had exchanged correspondences each other and met together in London in 1858. Anderson emphasized direct evangelism, aiming at the evangelization of the world, not at civilization. Anderson was optimistic with regard to the possibility of church planting, because he believed in the power of the Holy Spirit which gave vitality to the younger church. He held the conviction that evangelization would surely be followed by civilization. He saw missions as a spiritual conquest of the heathen. Henry Venn's fundamental concern was the planting of native churches supported by native peoples. He reacted negatively against the "mission church" concept which dominated missions of the eighteenth century. The nineteenth century was the age of paternalism and colonialism by the West. Accordingly, there was no idea of a church for the native people with native leaders in charge.

The Anglican churches (the Church of England) were reluctant to set up African ministers as bishops. Venn violently reacted against the dictatorial paternalistic fervor of Anglican churches. Venn's concern was the growth to maturity of the national church. As a matter of fact, the self-support principles are to be understood as an extension of Moravian missions, and Anthony Grove suggested this principle prior to Venn and Anderson. Anthony Norris Groves (1795-1853) was the first missionary who ignited the self-support principle theory; he was the pioneer missionary who suggested it and practiced himself. Groves has gone down in history as "the father of faith missions." His significance lies in his desire to simplify the task of churches and missions by returning to the methods of Christ and his apostles as described in the New Testament. As a missionary in India he put into practice the Apostle Paul's missions and suggested a return to the New Testament. He argued that the mission goal is to help indigenous converts form their own churches without dependence on foreign training, authorization or finance. His ideas eventually found wide acceptance in evangelical circles at that time. Groves had a major impact upon George Muller (who married Groves' sister Mary), and through him impacted James Hudson Taylor and many other significant Christian figures as well.

Most Mission Societies Adopted the Three Self-formula

The three self-formula is to be summarized as the planting of indigenous churches that were self-supporting, self-governing and self-propagating. The three self-formula was adopted by many missionary societies in the 19th century. In 1865, ABCFM made the following resolutions on the aim of mission: If we resolve the end of missions into its simplest elements, we shall find that it embraces: (1) the converting of lost men, (2) organizing them into churches, (3) giving those churches a competent native ministry, and (4) conducting them to the stage of independence and of self-propagation.[14] Occasionally, the labors of a missionary society will terminate when its church has become self-subsistent; but it must carry its work to the point of reliable self-development. For the ABCFM, the school and the press were to be regarded as auxiliaries; accordingly, education as an end can never be promoted. "Education, school, the press, and whatever else good to make up the working system, are held in strict subordination to the planting and building up of effective working churches. The governing object to be always aimed at, it self-reliant, effective churches –churches that are purely native."[15]   Oral preaching was to be absolutely indispensable, because without a living preacher the ultimate end of missions cannot be attained. Rufus Anderson exerted a great influence on all American missions. All the missionary agencies of the United States and Canada adopted most of the fundamental points of his policy. In England, the CMS and the London Missionary Society also adopted this principle as their aim of missions.

Nevertheless, the ABCFM had some weakness that they lacked a theological emphasis and their missions in Southeast Asia and Japan were said to be unsuccessful. The ABCFM did not come to Korea. In Japan, ABCFM contributed to establish the Japan Congregation Church as a denomination, however, this Churches theologically went to liberalism and the churches did not grow as much. Strangely many liberal theologians came from this Church; Among them Ebina Danjo was the first liberal theologian in Japan. His theology was known for Shintoistic Christianity. The Shintoism is a nationalistic religion of Japan that Japan is a chosen nation by the sun god *Amaterasuomikami*. His idea is that Christianity should provide the sense of justice and fairness of being a faithful citizen of Japan. He understood Christianity analogous to Confucianism. For him, Christ is not God, but a human who lived with strong religious consciousness. Christ is only divine in the sense that every person is divine. Later he attempted to bring Christianity in with line with Shintoism. He was one of the first theologians who adopted German biblical criticisms and liberal theology.[16] The ABCFM sent the first missionary to Thailand in 1834, but they closed the missions to Thailand for the poor results and the opening of China. A historian of the ABCFM, summarized discouraging growth as follows: "After a dozen years there was only one Siamese member of the Church, and he was suspended for a time; of the three Chinese members, one had gone to China, one had been an assistant to the mission, and one of the third it had to be said he does not run well."[17] Adoniram Judson was sent by the ABCFM to Myanmar, but he left the ABCFM to move to the Baptist Churches because of the issue of baptism. Later he has become a founding father of the Baptist Churches in Myanmar.

In 1837 the Old School Presbyterians left the ABCFM. The ABCFM was the first voluntary interdenominational mission society in America which was organized by the Congregational churches but many Presbyterians participated in it on individual basis. In the American Presbyterian churches, there was a division between the Old School Presbyterians and the New School Presbyterians. The Old School Presbyterians strongly adhered to the Reformed faith and theology of John Calvin. They contended that education and mission belong to the church, not independent mission society. Charles Hodge, as a Reformed theologian and leader of the Old School Presbyterianism, played an important role in organizing the Presbyterian Foreign Mission Board in 1837. Charles Hodge's view was in a striking contrast with to that of Anderson. He emphasized the organized churches, presbyteries, synods and General Assembly are the mission board. The Presbyterian Mission Board also adopted the self-support principles. "The supreme and controlling aim of foreign missions was to make the Lord Jesus known to all men as their Divine Savior and to persuade them to become his disciples; to gather their disciples into Churches which shall be self-propagating, self-supporting, self-governing; to cooperate, so long as necessary, with the Churches in evangelizing of their countrymen, and in bringing to bear on all human life the spirit and principles of Christ."[18] In Thailand, the first Presbyterian missionary, McGilvary, was a pioneer man. He attempted to practice the self-support principles by emphasizing the involvement of native workers to avoid dependence on missionary. However, the self-supporting principles were rejected by the native workers. The Baptist churches planted by the American Baptist missions were merged with the Presbyterian churches to organize the Church of Christ in Thailand (CCT). The present Baptist Convention was established by the Southern Baptist Churches in the twentieth century. The American Baptist missions in Myanmar was successful by the establishment of the Karen Baptist Church which became the first self-supporting church in Asia.

We would say in summary that the missions of the nineteenth century based their foundations on deep convictions concerning the word of God and the work of the Holy Spirit. Generally speaking, missionaries in the 19th century faithfully followed the exhortation of Paul: "I commend you to God and to the Word of His grace, which is able to build you up and to give you the inheritance among all those who are sanctified" (Acts 20:32).

The Karen Baptist Churches: A Model of Self-supporting Church

The Baptist missionaries concentrated their mission on the Buddhist Burmese people, but they found it too difficult to gain converts among the Burmese, so they concentrated their mission efforts on the animistic mountain tribal people, the Karen. The Karen were highly receptive to the Gospel. In 1860, at the Liverpool Mission conference several American Baptist missionaries reported about the Karen churches. The Karen were a people prepared by God to embrace the Gospel. A Baptist missionary in Myanmar reported about the Karen churches as follows:

> We pass on to Burma; and there we find rejoicing in the light and liberty of truth, 100,000 Karens; every one of whom, thirty years ago, was entirely ignorant of its very existence. There they are, meeting like ourselves on the Sabbath; working like ourselves for their ignorant brethren; supporting their pastors with the most active and self-denying zeal; contemplating the destitution of their heathen countrymen with compassion; and sending forth one and another of their brethren, with their lives in their hands to preach Christ among the barbarous tribes, still living in the mountains and the dense jungles of their wild land.[19]

Ecumenical Missions: Unity or Disunity?

The mission movements of the nineteenth century resulted in the ecumenical movements of the twentieth century; however, the ecumenical missions and liberal theologians de-evaluated the 19th century missions. In some ways it was like a son denying his mother. From the early twentieth century evangelical missions were condemned as representing religious imperialism, symbols of Western superiority, and lack of social concern. The nineteenth century patterns of mission, which were believed to be based on valid biblical principles, began to be criticized extensively by ecumenical missions. Some scholars in their research sought to track down the motives and the aims of all earlier mission activities.

The purpose of missions has become a debated issue in church and mission circles today. Many different views are held, and they seriously challenge the traditional view of mission. The aim of missions was standing at the crossroads of either "redemption" or "humanization". Beaver commented on the changing of the aim of mission: "Until at least the 1950's no American mission agencies or missionaries ever openly questioned Dr. Anderson's aim for the mission, namely, the fostering of self-propagating, self-governing, self-supporting churches."[20] Scherer said that for a hundred years missionary policy pursued a single goal – the planting of indigenous churches, but he denied its scriptural warrant in saying that this policy is not so obviously scriptural as it appears, nor does it solve all the problems of modern missions. The New Testament lays down no pattern for an indigenous church.

Some theologians suggested a pluralism in mission theory; namely, that the aim of missions is not only one definition, but plural definitions should be recognized. For instance, German missiologist Hans Margull boldly proposed to accept pluralism of views of mission in view of the complicated situation of the present time.[21] Peter Beyerhaus ascribed this plurality of views of mission to four reasons. First, with the liberation of Afro-Asian nations from colonial supremacy, the younger churches challenged the western church's ideas of missions. Second, the younger churches, recognizing the values of other religions in their countries, began to disassociate themselves from proselytism: the winning of people from one religious allegiance to another. Third, certain recent developments in western theology supported the

Asiatic inclination toward religious co-existence and syncretism. Fourth, the secularization of theology exerted a secularizing influence on mission.[22]

To introduce another view of missions, according to Barth, the objective of missions is not to convert heathen in the sense of bringing them to a personal enjoyment of their salvation. It is a proclamation that everyone has been already saved in Christ.[23] Paul Tillich, using the words "anonymous Christians" and "implicit Christianity", maintained that missions must be viewed as an attempt to transform the latent Church, in its hiddenness under the forms of paganism, Judaism and humanism, into its open manifestation. He rejected the traditional view of mission and expressed his position as follows:

> One should not misunderstand missions as an attempt to save from eternal damnation as many individuals as possible among the nations of the world. Such an interpretation of the meaning of missions presupposes a separation of individual from individual, a separation of the individual from the social group to which he belongs, and it presupposes an idea of predestination which actually excludes most human beings from eternal salvation and gives hope for salvation only to the few – comparatively few, even if it is millions – who are actually reached by the message of Jesus as the Christ. Such an idea is unworthy of the glory and of the love of God and must be rejected in the name of the true relationship of God to his world.[24]

Hans Hoekendijk, who exerted a profound influence on ecumenical missions, proposed shalom missions in place of the traditional view of *plantation ecclesia* as the aim of mission. His use of the term shalom was an attempt to concretize the concept of the Kingdom of God. This term is a secularized concept taken out of the religious sphere and used to indicate all aspects of restored and renovated human conditions: righteousness, truth, fellowship, communication, peace, etc., stating that "the evangelization of the heathen must be seen as a possibility only in the Messianic days."[25] Accordingly, Hoekendijk rejected the concept of preaching and the planting of the church since he felt these were not true to his Messianic conception of evangelism. Indian theologian M. M. Thomas also objected to the traditional conception of missions and designated it with the irresponsible judgment that "this approach has contributed to the Christian indifference to secular politics which led to the rise of Hitler and Stalin in the West."[26] James A. Scherer's, *Missionary, Go Home!*, was a disturbing volume in which he criticized certain aspects of the nineteenth century's mission efforts.

These criticisms seem to be very perceptive, but ecumenical missions by and large have shown the tendency to regard mission work in the nineteenth century as having been concerned only with the salvation of individual souls and having been associated with colonialism. When we carefully read their criticisms, we can understand in part what the dominant concept of nineteenth century mission was. Scherer defined the 19th century mission as cultural and ecclesiastical imperialism. He said that the nineteenth-century emphasis on moral and cultural uplift through missions was just as dangerous a displacement of the apostolic ideal as was the political motive. Missionaries came to the lands of Asia and Africa as representatives of a higher social order, convinced of the superiority of western civilization. Love for the sinner for whom Christ died degenerated easily into pity for the unfortunate and the backward.[27]

German missiologist Freytag concluded that 19th century missionary enthusiasm and action failed to preserve the force of the missionary motive as set forth in the Bible. His idea was that previously the Kingdom of God was the motive of missions, but in the 19th century the concept of the Kingdom of God was distorted or reduced into a narrow sense. Freytag was very critical to the Zinzendorf and the Moravian movement, stating that they narrowed down the Kingdom of God "to a purely spiritual and individualist-ethical outlook."[28]

These criticisms seem to be perceptive, but their mission theology must be verified from the Bible; these criticisms come from different views of the Scriptures. The aim of mission in the nineteenth century was that of presenting the truth which God has supernaturally recorded in the Bible rather than that of seeking truth together with adherents of other religions. Evangelicals believe that the Scriptures are the inspired and infallible Words of God. When we carefully read their criticisms, we learn that the critics of the 19th century missions distort the biblical concept of the missions. The ecumenical missions are too much preoccupied with social transformation, but without the individual regeneration, the social transformation is impossible. The 19th century missionaries realized this truth very well that "social reform in non-Christian communities must evolve out of deeper and more spiritual changes in the individual character."[29] The church does not exist primarily to satisfy the needs of the world, but rather it exists in the first place for God and his glory. Jesus Christ gave two commandments: the Great Commission and the Great Commandment. "All authority in heaven and on earth has been given to me. Therefore, go and make disciples of all nations" (Matt. 28:19) and "The Spirit of the Lord is on me, because he has anointed me to preach good news to the poor. He has sent me to proclaim freedom for prisoners and recovery of sight for the blind, to release the oppressed" (Luke 4:18). We quote Dr. John Stott who attempted to reconcile evangelical missions and the ecumenical missions: "There is another and particular responsibility which Christians have towards the world, as the Bible describes those outside Christ and his church: evangelism." [30] Civilization mission is said to have failed in conversion and church growth; however, it helped the nations open up to Christian mission. Nevertheless, civilization is so associated with colonialism that it led to resistance from the nationals, in that civilization could destroy the nation's longstanding cultural heritage and religion, the foundation of their civilization. In the nineteenth century the evangelical movements were optimistic that the light of the Christian faith would wipe out the dark religion of Asia, but it did not come true. Civilization mission, for example establishing schools and hospitals, demands tremendous funds. Civilization mission justified the need to employ native workers with money and to invest a lot of funds for buildings. But what happened in the mission fields after the missionaries left? While we refrain from mentioning other churches in Asia, we take an illustration from Korean churches: mission schools and hospitals are still involved in the property disputes among concerned leaders and pastors. A big mission hospital was eventually closed by the church which was the owner of the hospital. We define it as "money mission." K. P. Yohanan sharply criticizes: "To use God-given money to hire people to perpetuate our ways and theories is a modern method of old-fashioned imperialism."[31]

Endnotes

[1] J. Herbert Kane, *Understanding Christian Mission* (Grand Rapids: Baker Book House, 1975), 154.

[2] David Bosch, 258.

[3] Charles Hodge, *Systematic Theology*, vol. 1, 241.

[4] K. S.Latourette, *History of the Expansion of Christianity*, vol.5, (New York: Harper and Brothers, 1944), 496.

[5] James Dennis, 6.

[6] William Carey, "Carey on Witnessing A Sati," in *History of Christianity in India: Source Materials*, M. K. Kurikose, (compiled), (Madras: The Christian Literature Society, 1982), 72.

[7] William Bair & Bruce Hunt, *The Korean Pentecost* (Edinburg: Banner of Truth, 1977), 16.

[8] Onosizuo, *Nippon Protesutanto Dendousi* (Japanese) (*The Mission History of Japan*) (Hirosima: Reformed Church of Japan Pub., 1989),10- .

[9] Michael A. Laird, "The Legacy of Alexander Duff," *Occidental Bulletin of International Mission*, 3:4 (October 1979): 146.

[10] Michael A. Laird, 146.

[11] Church Missionary Society, *The Missionary Register for MDCC XVIII* (London: L. B. Seeley, 1818), 16.

[12] Eric S. Fife and Arthur F. Glaser, *Missions in Crisis: Rethinking Missionary Strategy*, (Chicago: Inter-Varsity Press, 1961), 55.

[13] James A. Dennis, vii.

[14] *Annual Report of the American Board of Commissioners for Foreign Missions.* October 31. 1856. 52.

[15] Rufus Anderson, *Foreign Missions: Their Relation and Claims* (New York: Charles Scribner and Co., 1869), 113.

[16] Yumi Murayama-Cain, "Japanese Church History: Historical Background and the Issue of Identity." *Humanistica e Theologia.* 31:2(2010): 221 203-244.

[17] Alex G. Smith, *Siamese God: The Church in Thailand* (Bangkok: OMF Pub., 1981), 24.

[18] Presbyterian Board, *The Modernism and the Board of Foreign Missions of the Presbyterian Church in the U. S. A.* (The Board of Foreign Missions of the Presbyterian Church in the U. S. A., 1033), 9.

[19] The Secretaries to the Conference, Conference on Missions Held in 1860 At Liverpool (London: James Nisbet, 1860), 307-308.

[20] R. P. Beaver, *To Advance the Gospel* (Grand Rapids: Eerdmans, 1967), 38.

[21] Hans Jochen Margull, "Mission '70 – More A Venture Than Ever," *International Review of Mission*, 60 (1971):57.

[22] Peter Beyerhaus, *Missions: Which Way* (Grand Rapids: Zondervan House, 1976), 18-21.

[23] Waldron Scott, "Karl Barth's Theology of Missions," *Missiology* 3: (April 1975): 216.

[24] Paul Tillich, "Mission and World History," in *Theology of the Christian Mission*, ed., Gerald Anderson, (New York: McGraw Hilll, 1961), 283-84.

[25] J. C. Hoekendijk, "The Call to Evangelism," in *The Conciliar – Evangelical Debates*, ed., Donald McGavran, (Pasadena: Willicam Carey Library, 1977), 46-47.

[26] M. M. Thomas, "Salvation and Humanization," *International Review of Mission*, 60 (1971):30.

[27] James A. Scherer, *Missionary, Go Home!* (Engelwood Cliffs: Prentice Hall, 1964), 33.

[28] Walter Freytag, The Meaning and Purpose of Christian Mission," *International Review of Mission*, 39:2 (1950): 154-55.

[29] James S. Dennis, *Christian Missions and Social Progress: A Sociological Study of Foreign Missions*, vol. 2. (New York: Fleming H. Revell, 1899), 7.

[30] John Stott, *Basic Christianity* (Grand Rapids: Eerdmans, 1971), 140.

[31] K. P. Yohanan, *Revolution in World Missions*, 206.

Chapter - 5

Christian Churches in Asia

About 50 years ago a Chinese evangelical and theologian, Lit Sen Chang, said that Christianity in Asia had succeeded in gaining a foothold but failed to get a heart hold. He accurately commented on Asian churches. The history of Christian missions has been long in Asia. Nevertheless, its growth is not so encouraging. At present the Christian churches in China, Singapore, Indonesia, and Nepal are growing despite severe persecution and suffering sometimes. Other churches in Asia seem to be stagnating. Every day in China 10,000 new converts come into the churches, even though Chinese churches are suffering under the Communist government oppression.

This chapter addresses the general situation of the Christian churches in Southeast Asia; largely focusing on the Indo-China nations comprising Vietnam, Cambodia and Laos. And for the purpose of this discussion Thailand and Myanmar will also be included. These five countries are generally characterized by one or more of the following facts – they practice Theravada Buddhism; they are developing countries; they are influenced by military regimes; and in the case of Vietnam and Laos they are Communist or Socialist nations. Christianity remains a small minority in this region despite its long history. Roman Catholic missions goes back to the early 16th century. However, Catholic churches are still very weak in this area.

Political democracy and freedom of religion are critical issues facing India and China. The reality of social, economic, religious and political enslavement causes massive human misery in this area. People are enslaved in the "cultural network" from which they could not escape. In Thailand "the land is held captive in a complex web of Buddhism, traditional culture, and spirit appeasement and even occult with a social cohesiveness out which few have dared to come."[1] Many people are victims of poverty. The countries of Indo-China are politically and socially unstable due to authoritative military regimes, social injustice, and corruption.

Churches in Asia

Conversion in Animistic Culture

We already mentioned that many Christians in Asia come from animistic tribal groups. In 1970 Stephen Neill suggested that 40 percent of the world's population based their lives on animistic thinking. In Myanmar majority Christians were animistic Karen, Aka, Hmong, and Lisu people. In India also majority were animistic in Nagaland and Mizoram. In Indonesia most animistic Batak and Kalimantan tribal people were head hunters. Now they have become Christians. The Philippines, Vietnam and Cambodia still are the mission fields of the Christian and Missionary Alliance (C&MA). The C&MA planted many churches in these countries. The Evangelical Church of Cambodia and Evangelical Church of Vietnam are the fruits of the C&MA. Fully 80% of the Evangelical Churches in Vietnam are from the animistic Hmong people on the mountain areas. The majority members of the Presbyterian churches in Vietnam come from animistic tribal groups on the mountain areas who needed permits from the police to come to cities.

Don Richardson, a pioneer heroic missionary who worked in Papua New Guinea, promoted a different idea. He suggested that animism has "native monotheism" despite many sprits and gods. Some missionaries observed that animism can become the point of contact for evangelism, because it has a faith in a monotheistic god (*Hananim* in Korea). In Korea the concept of Hananim (one god) has served as the point of contact for Korean Christians. If they become Christians, resistance and persecution from family or community is significantly weaker compared to the Buddhist, Hindu and Islamic cultures.

Ethnic-Oriented Church

Racism is a major factor in ethnic conflicts in Southeast Asia. Ethnic-oriented church is so influenced by cultural exclusivities that they often don't attempt evangelism towards other ethnic groups. Many minority groups especially detest the dominant group because the dominant often look down upon the minority groups. So, we cannot expect the Gospel message to be readily shared between the dominant and minority groups. Dominant people groups also are hesitant to hear from the people of minority groups or uneducated people. The countries of Indo-China are ethnically and linguistically multiple society. So, the central government puts their efforts for all minority group people to speak the national language. However, many minority churches preach in their tribal language. Plus, they publish Christian literature and Bible study materials in their own language. So, a pastor who preaches in the national language is under pressure from the same ethnic leaders. Many churches in the big cities are not ethnic-oriented in which diverse ethnic peoples come together beyond ethnicity. We think in Myanmar the ethnic-oriented churches do not make a contribution to national unity, and it can even lead to church division. We want to take an illustration from the Myanmar Baptist Churches: In Myanmar there are many Baptist sub-groups by the ethnic groups: the Karen Baptist Church, The Kachin Baptist Church, etc. However, they are under one umbrella of the Myanmar Baptist Convention. They are the same God's covenant people. The Christian identity should be a priority over the national and political identity. We already pointed out that an ethnic-oriented denomination church is not biblically validated. In the Bible, the title of local church was given by the locality, not by the ethnicity: The Church of Antioch, the Church of Rome, and the Church of Ephesus.

Our suggestion is that an ethnic-oriented church can be justified if an ethnic local church can lead their same ethnic people to Christ. Our idea rests on Dr. MaGavran's homogenous unit principle and the people's movement. The homogenous unit principle and people movement were suggested by Donald D. McGavran in 1930s in India. The homogenous unit principle is that a church must consist of an ethnic group's people. The people's movement means that an ethnic group people simultaneously convert to Christ through the people's group decision. McGavran contended that "the early Church was made up of Jews only. It was a one-people Church for some years. the ethnic-oriented church.[2] His idea is that if the church consists of diverse people, the church growth would be slow. The case of the people's movement is that the peoples of northern Europe came to Christian faith in group movements. First one tribe would be discipled and then some years later or centuries later another tribe would find a Christ ward movement being born within it. Christendom arise out of

People Movements.[3] McGavran's emphasis is not an individual becoming a Christian, but *Peoples* become Christian.

McGavran's is that an ethnic group's church should be a bridge of God through which the same people convert to Christ. In other word, an ethnic people church is a means for the evangelization of the same ethnic people. We do not hear that the people movement is taking place in Southeast Asia. We know that in 1980s the Hmong people in Vietnam have become Christians through the Gospel messages from the Far East Christian Broadcast.

In this section we would like to suggest that the unreached people movement's mission policy need to be changed in Southeast Asia. The role of Christian churches is demanded to become a peacemaker. It is not desirable for a minority ethnic church to insist only their language. The unreached people movement mission strategy came from McGavran and Ralph Winter of the Fuller seminary. Their policy is that a missionary should use only their ethnic language to preach the Gospel. But Dr. James who is conducting a regular meeting with the Shan people in Chiang Mai communicates in Thai language. According to him, most Shan people in Chiang Mai speak bilingual of Shan and Thai for their survival in Thailand. He contributed an article to the magazine of Unreached People Movement. In the article he suggested to change the mission strategy of the unreached People movement who insists only tribal language. He argues that the Shan people in Chiang Mai "typically have a command of the Thai language as a result of the upbringing in Thailand, and a command of Thai written language as a result of schooling."[4]

Independent Local Church

There are many independent local churches in Asia. Independent local churches are not affiliated with denominations or church groups. The leaders of independent churches justify their policy of independence by claiming that denominational churches lack church purity and integrity. We need to notice that independent local churches have more problems. The most serious problem of independent local churches today arises from mishandling of the church property. Frequently, the leaders of independent local churches do not consider very seriously that church property should be legally corporate in character. Traditionally church property is registered with the local government as the personal property of the pastor. We saw many cases in Cambodia where church property left by missionaries was taken by an individual pastor or lay-leader.

The pastor of an independent local church does not seriously consider the fellowship and unity with other Christian community and churches. We confess to believe in a holy catholic church. The Church of Christ is one, holy, and catholic (universal). Many independent pastors do not have regular theological education and Bible training. Doctrinal and expository preaching may be difficult for them. It is almost impossible to expect accurate biblical preaching based on an exact and comprehensive understanding of the Bible.

Poor Church and Dependency

The most pressing issue facing Christian churches in Asia is their poverty and dependence on foreign assistance. Majority of Christians come from the lower or poor class. So, though they have outside jobs to support the family, they are compelled to accept foreign assistance to survive. Some large denominational churches practice inter-aid: large churches helping poor churches within their denomination. However independent poor churches only depend on foreign money. If foreign dependency lasts for a long time, it distorts the spiritual perspectives of both the giving and receiving churches.

Many churches have been planted by foreign missionaries with financial aid. Some churches have existed already for more than 20 years, yet there is no promising sign of becoming self-supporting. We confess that many Korean missionaries are also guilty of maintaining this unhealthy dynamic. The writer admits he cried about this impediment and advocated to Korean missionaries in the seminary to "Throw the baby into the river so that he will learn to swim by himself." Paul committed the church of Ephesus to God with these words, "Now I commit you to God and to the word of his grace, which can build you up and give you an inheritance among all those who are sanctified" (Acts:20:32). Paul himself was a tentmaker who avoided undue financial dependency (Acts 18:3).

Even in the rich nation there are many poor churches who failed to become a self-supporting church. Nevertheless, many pastors do not depend on other churches, they are working in secular jobs. In Korea more than 70% of the churches are not financially self-supporting. Most Korean local churches are affiliated with a denomination. Neighboring churches in the same denomination systematically help economically the weak church. For instance, the largest Presbyterian Church of *Tonghap* groups (WCC member church) stipulated a rule that every pastor of the member church serving in a local church to receive minimum salary. Then how could the headquarter of the Church provide minimum salary to every local church? The large churches are obliged to send the designated money to the presbytery (an organization unit of a regional churches). The presbytery would then give the money to the local pastor. This is the biblical principle of coexistence. The independent local church system could not practice such a system.

WCC divides the Churches

Most mainline denominational churches in Asia have been divided into evangelicals and liberals after the formation of the World Council of Churches (WCC). The WCC is a Christian organization dedicated to the search for Christian unity. It is a voluntary fellowship of churches which confess the Lord Jesus Christ as God and Savior. The WCC "seeks visible unity in one faith and promotes common witness in work for mission and evangelism; engage in Christian service by meeting human needs, breaking down barriers between people, seeking justice and peace, and upholding the integrity of creation." Unfortunately, the church union movement resulted in church division: in Korea the several mainline churches of Presbyterian, Methodist, and Evangelical Churches (Holiness Churches) have been divided into the conservatives and the liberal groups. In Myanmar the Baptist Churches planted by the evangelical American Baptist missionaries split into the evangelical Baptist and the "progressive" Baptists. In Thailand there was division between the Christian Church of Thailand affiliated with the WCC and the Evangelical Fellowship of Thailand.

The origin of the WCC ecumenical movement goes back to the Edinburgh Mission Conference in 1910 which is the birthplace of the modern ecumenical movement. If we express the objectives of the WCC in two words, they would be unity and mission. These words are meant to be understood as two sides of the same coin. But it is well-known that mission has almost been missing in many WCC churches and mission organization. In 1957 the Christian Conference of Asia (CCA) was organized as a regional organization. The Conference discussed missionary obligation of the Christian church. However, more emphasis seems to have been given to social concern than to evangelism.

Challenges of Cults

Asian Christian churches are facing crucial threats from many cults (counterfeit Christianity, heresy). Major cultic groups in Asia largely come from the United States and Korea, some from Taiwan and China. These sects claim to be another Christian denominational church and take weak Christians away from true Christian churches. They are more passionate in evangelism than the orthodox Christian churches. For American cult missionaries, English is a strong and effective weapon to attract young people and students to English language classes. They are very dedicated in their mission work and are always smartly dressed and very wholesome in appearance. The Church of Jesus Christ of Latter-day Saints (Mormons), claim to have 14,000 followers in Cambodia, they have the funds to build multi-million-dollar buildings, and their humanitarian donations have gained them praise and respectability by the highest levels of the Cambodian government.[5]

The Korean cults *Shinchonjii* (new heaven and earth), Salvation group, and the Church of Good, are also great challenges to the churches in Southeast Asia and in Korea. The followers of these cult claim to be good Christians, but they are deceived by brainwashing from the cult teachers. The cults deny essential Christian doctrines such as Sola Scriptura, the deity of Christ, the Trinity, and salvation by grace through faith instead of by works. For example, the Korean cult *Shinchonji,* known as Church of Jesus, was founded in 1984 by ex-evangelical Lee Man-hee. Shincheonji, is translated as "New Heaven and Earth," and falsely claims that Jesus is a spirit entity that entered the body of Lee, who now claims unique understanding of the Bible and apocalypse. Lee claims that he is a prophet superseding Jesus. Lee claims the world has already ended, that we are all in the afterlife, that he will live forever, and that all other churches are controlled by

Satan. Some people argue that the emergence of cults is responsible for the Churches, but we learn from Scripture that the cults (heresy) appeared in the early Churches. They threatened the churches newly planted by the Apostles and the disciples of Jesus Christ.

Jesus Christ warned of the appearance of false Messiah at the end of the time: "Watch out that no one deceive you. For many will come in my name, claiming I am Christ" (Matt. 24:4-5). The Apostle Paul warned the Church in Galatia to watch out for the Judaists who were imposing Judaic regulations on the Gentile converts: "Those who want to impress people by means of the flesh are trying to compel you to be circumcised. The only reason they do this is to avoid being persecuted for the cross of Christ. Not even those who are circumcised keep the law, yet they want you to be circumcised that they may boast about your circumcision in the flesh" (Gal. 6:12-13). The cultic groups deny the divinity of Jesus Christ. "I say this because many deceivers, who do not acknowledge Jesus Christ as coming in the flesh, have gone out into the world. Any such person is the deceived.

Church Leadership

Leadership building is an urgent task for the Asian Churches. Definition of leadership differs from the East and the West, and it differs from culture to culture. Secular leadership and Christian leadership are different and should be different. Secular leadership tends to become ruler-oriented. The exercise of leadership is generally culturally conditioned. Asian culture is elder-oriented society. Thus, leader exercises paternalistic leadership which require that the subject should follow elder and leader unconditionally. Obedience to the elder or leader is a good virtue. However, Christian leadership is entirely different. We read it in the Bible: "The kings of the Gentiles lord it over them; and those who exercise authority over them call themselves Benefactors. But you are not to be like that. Instead, the greatest among you should be like the youngest, and the one who rules like the one who serves." (Lk. 22:25-26). In Romans 12: 8 says that leadership is a spiritual gift: "If is with leadership, let him govern diligently." Paul teaches us that "the elders who direct the affairs of the church well are worthy of double honor" (I Tim. 5:17).

Bill Lawrence defines Christian leadership as follows: "Leadership is the act of influencing /serving others out of Christ's interests in their lives so they accomplish God's purposes for and through them." He suggests seven virtues of Christian leadership: love, modesty, self-development, motivation, correction, integrity, and follower of God's will.[6] In this regard the Asian churches demand a good exercise of leadership. Dr. John Davies an OMF missionary in Thailand has once criticized the authoritarian ministry of the Hmong Church, the Yao Church, and the Korean Church pastors. The mis-behaviors of a few leaders in the mega-church of Korea and Singapore have been largely reported in the secular mass media. We believe that it does a great damage to the Christian churches of the two countries.

Our urgent question is: How does secular society view the pastor of the Church in Asia? It is a very significant question. Max Weber once visited America for a survey why American churches were growing in the nineteenth century. He concluded that the revival of the American church is deeply related to good reputations of the pastors of American churches. Buddhism monk and Islam imam hold sway in Buddhism and Islamic culture by nature of their status. The majority churches in Asia are the denomination church of historical Christianity. However, there are many churches of the small group led by a church leader. The lay preacher or minister of this small group church do not have a regular theological training in well-established theological institution or seminary school. They are trained by their leader. The leader invites his pastors on a regular basis for teaching and fellowship. We see many good leaders in the Asian churches. But leadership crisis is the crisis of the Asian churches, The Asian Christian churches are surrounded by the hostile environment. So, the church absolutely needs a unity and cooperation among the church leaders.

Theological Education and Ministry

Theological schools in Southeast Asia are still in a relatively poor situation in terms of faculties, facilities, curriculum development, student quality, and library. Many governments in Asia do not recognize the existence of seminaries. Vietnam churches are in critical need of more seminaries and Bible schools to train church workers and ministers, but the government does not allow new seminaries. This is the reason for underground schools. In Laos there are 500 Protestant churches and 150,000 Christian without seminary at all. In contrast, Myanmar is alleged to have too many seminary and Bible schools.

An urgent task in theological education and in ministry is how to deal with the shortage of Christian materials. Many pastors and seminary students rely only on the Bible and poor guidebooks with pictures. The guidebooks for the Bible are in abundance. The students are not equipped enough to understand high level lectures. Students do not have a basic understanding of Philosophy, World history and Christian history. So, it is difficult to explain to them about such terms as enlightenment, rationalism, Deism, and Neo-orthodox theology. In 2010 Cambodia Presbyterian Theological Institute adopted the Theological Statements that professors can teach or introduce biblical criticism and Neo-orthodox theology.

However,great caution must be exercised because students find it hard to understand "new theology" based on the dialogical logics, liberalism, and philosophy of the West.

The WCC developed contextualized theology relevant to Asian culture and society. The theological institutes supported by the WCC are more advanced in terms of the academic level, professor, and facility. The Theological Education Fund (TEF) has played a major role in it. Nevertheless, we point to ecumenical theology as a problem. In 1973 Dr. Shoki Coe the director of the TEF suggested the application of contextualized theology to theological education in Asia, and conducted a research work on theological education in Asia and urged that liberation theology be taught in the seminary schools. The WCC theology is more concerned with social issues such as the violation of human rights, exploitation, injustice, corruption, poverty, and environmental problems. Could teaching liberation theology in Asia be compared to setting fire on oil? We suppose that many countries are in fragile because of oppression, corruptions and dictatorial regimes.

We would take an example: In Indonesia the theology of religious pluralism is now a forbidden subject. Muslims have strong conviction that only Islam is the absolute true religion. The books on pluralism theology are preserved in special section in the library which is closed to the students. Theological liberalism places their emphasis to the term "relevance." Radical theology is not relevant to the situation of Asia. We have already learned from the history that revolution has failed to transform nations and society. Only regenerated man with the words of God and the Holy Spirit can transform a person and the world. The French revolution is the history of the failure of revolution. Only regenerated ones could change a society.

We suggest that the seminary in Asia teach the theology of religion not liberation theology. The tragedy of the Killing Fields should be examined not only from the political and social perspectives but also from a religious perspective. We already mentioned Pol Pot in the chapter 2, but we need to notice that Pol Pot hated Buddhism and killed more Buddhists than Christians. An Indonesian theologian pointed out the ambivalent function of religion, both the positive and negative side of religion. He argued that religion can become the potential for positive social change, while "in its sociologically enslaving face, it tends to legitimize an oppressive status quo."[7] We rarely hear that the local religion implemented social or political reform. The term reform or reformation may be a prohibited word in this culture.

Regrettably, modern theologians generally dismiss the negative sides of other religions, and they are only eager to have a dialogue and cooperation with other religions. Dialogue theology suggests inter-religious cooperation with other religions by holding inclusive views of salvation. We agree that the attitude of condemnation or condescension towards communities of other faiths is inappropriate and would only disable Christians from making a meaningful witness to the rest of the religion. But what is needed is inter-religious cooperation in secular issues of community development and anti-criminal campaign, not an unholy compromise of Scripture. Evangelical theology rejects the inclusivism model of salvation, the un-biblical notion that everyone is already saved in Christ without ever repenting of sin and confessing Jesus as the Lord and Savior. Theologians define this inclusivism model as Neo-universalism. We do not agree with the neo-Orthodox theology of Karl Barth and Emil Brunner. One does not deny the eternal truth of Scripture in order to obtain temporal unity between conflicting religions.

We emphasize the need to develop Christian apologetics that are specially designed for Asia, because pastors preach to people of various other religions (1 Pet. 3:15). We want to propose missionary apologetics as suggested by German missiologist Gustav Warneck.[8] He debated with Ernst Troeltsche, who was a theologian of *Religiongeschichte Schule* (school of religion history) in Germany. Warneck rejected Troeltsche's pluralist model and suggested to defend fundamental Christian truths in reasonable persuasion and evangelism in a humble attitude, but not concession or surrender to other religions (II Tim. 2:24-26).

Theological seminaries need to teach the subject "power encounter." Theological definition of power encounter is a spiritual war between the kingdom of God and the kingdom of evil power (Satan). Many a minster do not know how to deal with demon possession person in the church. The encounter of Moses with king Pharaoh and that of Elijah with the Baal prophets are a good illustration of power encounter as found in Ephesians 6:10-12: "Finally, be strong in the Lord and in his mighty power. Put on the full armor of God, so that you can take your stand against the devil's schemes. For our struggle is not against flesh and blood, but against the rulers, against the authorities, against the powers of this dark world and against the spiritual forces of evil in the heavenly realms."

People in Buddhism and animistic culture are afraid of ghost or spirits. Even in America where the spirits or ghosts are theologically dismissed the demonology has been developed long time ago. Buddhism is syncretized with animism in Southeast Asia. So, the Buddhists are afraid that if they change their religion, they will be punished by the spirits. Liberal theology is not much concerned with the spiritual dimensions of angels, satanic ghosts which are placed between the spiritual world of God and Heaven and the world. Paul Hiebert defines it as the "excluded middle" neglected in the West. In this regard; there is a polarization between evangelicals and liberals in theological education. Liberal seminary curricula focus more on social issues (sociology), while evangelical seminary curricula are more concerned with the authority of Scripture in reference to culture (anthropology) and religions. Liberal theology tends to dismiss the practical aspects related with the spiritual world. Even Christians in Southeast Asia tend to think that diseases always come from evil spiritual powers. Sometimes Sunday worship services arrange special prayer time for sick persons and lay-preachers, or pastors lay hands on them with prayer. Many ministers are involved in spirit-oriented ministry. Taken to extreme, this also represents some danger of deviation from biblical Christianity.

Christianity was born in Asia as an Asian religion; it began its mission work from Asia. Yet, here it still remains a minority religion. Some Asian countries are deporting Christian missionaries. Perhaps Korean missionaries are in a most difficult situation because Korea is now the second largest missionary sending nation next to America. Christian churches in Indo-China do not enjoy full freedom of faith. Cultural and social environment keep people from converting to Christianity. Despite opposition, the Christian churches in some nations are growing and demonstrate the power of Christ's presence in their nation and societies.

Nevertheless, the churches in Indo-China are facing stagnation in church growth, leadership crisis, negative influences of liberal theology, a crisis regarding how to improve theological education, and a desperate need for effective evangelism and discipleship. But the most urgent task is how to help poor and weak churches to stand on their feet in Christ, be freed from the relation between sponsor and clients, so that the churches and mission organizations can attain and maintain equal and respectful partnership with each other.

Finally, our ultimate question: is it possible to transform the Gentile nations into a Christian value system? However, every Christian church must be united to evangelize the nations of Southeast Asia with the salvation message. "And this gospel of the kingdom will be preached in the whole world as a testimony to all nations, and then the end will come" (Matt. 24:14).

Endnotes

[1] "Transform World: Global Challenges Summit 2012," (unpublished materials presented in Transform World Conference in Bali, November 2012): 54.

[2] Donald A. McGavran, *The Bridge of God: A Study in Strategy of Missions* (New York: Friendship Press, 1955), 18.

[3] Donald McGavran, 38.

[4] James D. Langteau, Ho Jin Jun, Kenneth Gossett, and Dina Samora, "Peace Mission to Karen and Shan Migrants from Myanmar in Southeast Asia," *International Journal of Frontier Missiology*, 30: 1 Spring 2019:23.

[5] Julie Masis, "Mormons on the March," December 7, 2010. *Asia Times Online* http://www.atimes.com/atimes/Southeast_Asia/LL07Ae01.html

[6] "What is Christian leadership," https//online.campbellsville.edu/ministry/Christian-leadership-principle.

[7] A. A. Yeyangoe, *Theologia Crucis in Asia* (Amsterdam: Rodopy, 1987), 16-17.

[8] Gustav Warneck, *Evangelische Missionslehre*, 3 Abt., (Friedrich Andreas Perthes, 1903), 125-28.

Chapter 6

Early Korean Missions

Korea was a hermit nation closed to the outside world prior to the arrival of Western missionaries. The country was uncivilized without modern government, education systems, hospitals, and well-developed public institutions. The government did not allow missionaries to freely operate in the country; however, eventually through pressure from Western powers the door for missions was opened. In geopolitics, Korea was a nation sandwiched between the countries of China, Russia and Japan. At the time, the United States and Britain supported Japan's occupation of the Korean peninsula in order to deter Russia's southward policy. As mentioned in Chapter 1, the German theologian Gustav Warneck supported Japan occupied Korea for evangelization and modernization. However, history proves that Japan's occupation of Korea resulted in the division of South and North Korea after the Second World War. An American journalist, Michael Breen, rightly analyzed the political situation at that time: "The loss of national independence offered a compelling impetus to accept the Western faith: Confucianism had failed the Koreans, and this Western religion stood in opposition to the Japanese. Conversion was therefore acceptable both as a kind of penance for Korean failure and as patriotic commitment to a better future. Churches were also effective. Until the eve of World War Two, they remained the only institutions not subordinated to the Japanese."[1] The Chinese culture has made a strong impact on Korea in terms of religion, government systems, education and customs. Confucianism, which is a symbol of Chinese culture, became a state religion for 5 hundred years in the Yi Dynasty. Confucianism is so conservative that reforming and changing the status quo is almost condemned as a betrayal to tradition and widely held value systems. It makes it difficult to accept a new religion and ideology. Christianity and modernization have resulted in a radical change in Korea and contributed to the nation's modernization.

Korea Missions: Continuity with the 19th Century Missions

The concept of missions in Korea was a continuation of the evangelical missions of the nineteenth century. Many early American missionaries were greatly impacted by the Great Awakening and student revival movements in America. Their object in missions was to save the Korean people from eternal perdition. From its inception, their missions' concept of salvation is clear-cut: believing in Jesus to be saved from sins and to become a new man in Christ. The Korean mission has been dominated by American Presbyterian missions whose theology was a traditional form of Calvinism. The American Methodist missionaries were also typical evangelicals who accepted the Bible as the inspired and infallible word of God. An American sociologist, Spencer J. Palmer, defined the early faith of Korean Christians as "Puritanical ethic and Wesleyan zeal of evangelism."[2] The Presbyterian missionaries intended to establish a "native Church holding to the Reformed Faith and the Presbyterian form of government" from the very beginning of their mission works in Korea. Through establishing schools and hospitals, they made great contributions to the modernization of Korean society.

However, these institutions were only the means to an end. It is said that the missionaries were so intent upon their evangelistic work that the application of the gospel to social and economic conditions was minimized. Brown, General Secretary of the North Presbyterian Mission Board, describes the characteristics of the early Korean church as follows:

> The typical missionary of the first quarter century after the opening of the country was a man of the Puritan type. He kept the Sabbath as our New England forefather did a century ago. He looked upon dancing, smoking, and card-playing as sins in which no true follower of Christ should indulge. In theology and biblical criticism, he was strongly conservative, and he held as a vital truth the pre-millenarian view of the second coming of Christ. Higher criticism and liberal theology were deemed dangerous heresies. In most of the evangelical churches of America and Great Britain, conservatives and liberals have learned to live and work together in peace; but in Korea the few men who hold "the modern view" have a rough road to travel, particularly in the Presbyterian group of missions.[3]

His comments display little sympathy with the theology of the American missionary. It is true that the Korean church was characterized by Puritan ethics and conservative theology rejecting biblical criticism and liberalism. Liberal theology came to Korea after the year 1920 through the Japanese churches. The early Korean churches demonstrate that only an evangelical view of the Scriptures can bring about church growth. As early as 1910, 25 years after the start of missions in Korea, the Edinburgh Missionary Conference reported that the growth of the church in Korea had been "marvelous."[4] In this respect early Korean missions was much different from Chinese and Japanese missions to which the Western missionaries brought liberal theology from the beginning.

In the early Korean missions, missions run by denominations succeeded more than those run by para-church organizations. In Korea, interdenominational mission agencies did not arrive before World War II. So, from its inception, the Korean churches became doctrine and confession-oriented churches, and Sunday worship was presided only by an ordained pastor. We suggest that the early Korean missions could be a good model for modern missions in terms of fellowship, cooperation and unity among missionaries beyond denominations.

Early Korean Missions

Unity and Cooperation

From the outset, the missionaries did their best to avoid competition and discord among themselves. The earlier missionaries from different denominations realized well the benefits of a truly ecumenical and co-operative pattern of work, and they were unwilling to divide over non-essential denominational differences. Four Presbyterian missions of the North American Presbyterian, South American Presbyterian, Australian Presbyterian, and Canadian Presbyterian, and two Methodist Churches (North American Methodist and South Methodist Church) organized the General Council of Protestant Evangelical Missions in Korea with the purpose of establishing one evangelical Korean Church. The plan was not accomplished, but the comity system came out later. Bruce F. Hunt, the Orthodox Presbyterian missionary to Korea, who was branded as a separatist by the missionaries of ecumenical orientation, recognized this ecumenical spirit in the early Korean mission as follows: "Those early missionaries were not ignorant of the claims of a true ecumenicity on their attention, and they were rightly anxious not to bring to Korea allegedly Christian practices from the West which were merely accidental to the Christian faith and not a part of the real essence of Christianity. They properly wished not to bring in unessential denominational differences."[5]

The Comity System

A very important characteristic of the Korean mission was the comity system which was first suggested and then adopted by the Presbyterian Churches and, later by the Methodist Churches. In 1889, four Presbyterian Missions formed the Presbyterian Council, which acted as the ruling ecclesiastical body for the emerging Church in Korea. In 1893, the Council of Missions was formed. Its object was "the uniform organization in Korea of but one native church holding the Reformed Faith and the Presbyterian Form of Government."[6] In the face of such an attractive objective, the four Presbyterian missions speedily drafted comity agreements and laid plans for functional cooperation among themselves. The field agreement of 1892 assigning Chula Province in the south to the Presbyterian Church in the U.S. was accepted by a joint conference of representatives of the two Boards in New York. When the Canadian Presbyterian Mission arrived in Korea an agreement was made with the Northern Presbyterian Mission and it was assigned the two east coast Ham Kyong Provinces. Busan was turned over to the Australian mission in 1910, and the whole of South Kyongsang Province in 1913. The Northern Presbyterian Mission retained the other areas where it had been at work, with the approval of the three Presbyterian bodies mentioned above. As early as 1907, a Presbytery of the Korean Presbyterian Church was organized through the cooperation of these four Presbyterian Missions in accordance with the policy of the Council of Mission.

Later, these four Presbyterian missions agreed to a sharing of their territory with the Methodists. To achieve a pattern of friendly cooperation with the Methodist Church, the General Council of Protestant Evangelical Missions in Korea was organized in 1905. This General Council arose out of resolutions adopted in 1895, by a Joint Committee of representatives of the four Presbyterian and two Methodist organizations. The aim of the Council was cooperation in Mission efforts and eventually the organization in Korea of but one native evangelical Church.

This Council stressed the importance of unity to the Korean church. It made Korean Christians aware of their essential oneness in Jesus Christ. The early missionaries taught the Korean churches that the church is holy and catholic (universal) by not keeping the younger church in isolation from other churches outside Korea. Indeed, they sought to contact with a wide range of international gatherings and organizations from Edinburgh 1910 to Nairobi 1975. At the beginning, the missionaries largely dominated the international meetings of these churches, but from Jerusalem Council 1928 onward, the national leaders became increasingly involved in international mission conferences. These contacts have had a great influence on ecumenical perspectives within the Korean Church.

The General Council of the Evangelical Missions played an important role in an extensive evangelistic movement known as the "Million Movement." From 1905 to 1909 a Great Awakening swept over the Korean Church; this eventually led to the generation of an evangelistic movement. In 1909, the General Council decided to participate in this latter effort by adopting the slogan, "A million souls for Christ." In this way from the very beginning, ecumenical involvement in Korea had a close relationship with evangelism. However, this involvement was not merely a pragmatic coming together for the purpose of sharing a common task. We should especially note that this ecumenical activity came from strong feelings of spiritual unity. Horace G. Underwood, the first Presbyterian missionary, confirmed this when he wrote, "A deep feeling of spiritual unity prevailed, all hearts were melted, denominational distinctions seemed less important, and a passionate desire for the union of all the Christian forces in Korea dominated every mind."[7]

In this respect, J. Edwin Orr also agreed that the ecumenical movement in the Korean Church was the result of a prior spiritual awakening.[8] However, it should be noted that some people of the group in the Korean Church hotly attacked the comity system on the grounds that it generated both provincialism and church division. This criticism is not reasonable, because provincialism in Korea had a long history before the coming of the missionaries, and church division did not take place along the provinces; rather it was due to the issues of liberal theology, the Shinto Shrine, and church politics.

In summary, it should be underscored that the comity system was the beginning of the ecumenical movement in the Korean Church. Later, this led to the organization of the Korea National Council of Churches (KNCC).

Mission Strategy: Nevius Method

The early Presbyterian missionaries might have had their own missionary ideas and policies, but they were unable to translate it into workable practice in this new field. So, they invited John L. Nevius, a missionary with the Presbyterian Board in China, to help them. They learned from him the missionary methods which he had used in Shantung province of China. Nevius put emphasis on Bible study and the self-support of each individual church. Nevius developed his methods from analyzing the failure of what he called the "Old Method" in China, which involved depending on paid native agents to carry out all evangelistic work. The "rice Christians" has become a famous negative word to express the Christians converted through an impure motive of money. This term appeared first in China. Many missionaries in China employed native agents for spreading the Gospel and Nevius realized that financial support might endanger and even paralyze the young Church's growth, not only towards autonomy, but also towards the full sense of responsibility for evangelism. The basic themes of the Nevius method are summarized by Dr. Allen Clark as follows:

1. Missionaries should engage in evangelism with wide itineration.

2. The Bible must be central in every part of the work.

3. Self-propagation: every believer should be a teacher of someone else, and a learner from someone else better fitted; every individual and group should seek by the "layering method" to extend the work.

4. Self-government: every group should be under its chosen unpaid leaders; circuits under their own paid helpers, who will later yield to Pastors; circuit meeting training the people for later district, provincial and national leadership.

5. Self-support: with all chapels provided by the believers; each group, as soon as founded, beginning to pay towards the circuit helper's salary; that only when being founded; no pastors of single churches provided by foreign funds.

6. Systematic Bible study for every believer under his group leader and circuit helper; and every leader and helper in the Bible classes.

7. Strict discipline enforced by appealing to Bible standards.

8. Co-operation and union with other bodies, or at least territorial division.

9. Non-interference in lawsuits or any such matters.

10. General helpfulness where possible in the economic problems of the people.[9]

This system was applied to the Korean Church from the very beginning, "although, in the development of these ideas, local conditions and our experience in adapting the methods to meet different circumstances have led to great modification."[10] These principles as adopted by the Korean mission display what might be called typical characteristics of nineteenth century missions with their emphasis on the Bible, the saving of individual souls, and the strict discipline of believers. Latourette comments: "A striking feature of the methods employed by Protestant missions in Korea was the emphasis upon the participation of national believers in the spread of the Christian message and upon the financial self-support of the churches from the very beginning."[11]

Dr. Nevius applied the self-support, self-propagation, and self-government of Rufus Anderson and Henry Venn to the Korean churches. However, he specifically emphasized self-support as per the poverty-stricken condition of Korea to avoid the mistakes in China. The first Churches were erected at Sorai and Chemulpo with contributions made by Korean Christians. Most church buildings in Korea, with some exceptions, were constructed without foreign money.

Korean Christians have not been allowed to expect paid employment from the missionaries. As far as church houses go the edifice is usually a very humble one; but it is as good as the houses in which the members live, and sometimes it is the most notable building in the community. The people prize it because it belongs to them. The most competent man among them is selected as their leader, and he is responsible for the conduct of the work without compensation. The missionary visits these outstations once or twice a year to give such counsel and supervision as may be needed; but at all other times the Christians manage their own affairs.

The self-supporting principle was extended to schools, Bible distribution, and hospitals. The financial assistance given by the Mission was only about one-twentieth of the contributions of the Church for congregational expenses. Poverty had nothing to do with the question of self-support. The faith in the justice of self-support gave them the power to accomplish the evangelical mandate in planting the younger church.

The Nevius method can be summarized into two principles, emphasizing self-support of the church and Bible study. Nevius followed the pattern of St. Paul who left the converts to God and the work of his grace when he departed the church that he planted and served for almost 3 years. Without Bible study, we doubt if the plan could be a success, since without it the church would be spiritually starved. Early missionaries believed that the greatest secret of the great growth of the Church was Bible study. The missionaries and the Korean Christians accepted the Bible as a book of authority and a source of spiritual vitality, and they had clear-cut creedal statements which lay down definite standards and tests which can be applied by less qualified group leaders and helpers. Dr Allen Clark believed that the study of the Bible would be the key to the success of self-support, self-propagation, and self-government.

Revival Movement: Korean Pentecost

In 1907, the revival movements coincided with the revival movements in Wales, India and the United States. The revival movement took place as the results of Bible classes and prayers of repentance from the missionaries and Korean Christians. The revival movement was started by a Methodist missionary, Thomas Hardie, who was a medical doctor ministering in Kangwon province of North Korea. He reflected seriously on his mission works and prayed in repentance for his pride and hardness of heart against other missionaries. At a Bible study he had an extraordinary experience of the Holy Spirit. This repentance movement reached a large scale, with Bible studies occurring among several hundred attendants in a Church in Pyongyang, now the capital city of North Korea. It is meaningful that at that time the London Times compared the explosion of the Holy Spirit in Korea with the revival of John Wesley:

> You have only to read the journal of John Wesley and compare it with the account of the manifestation Pyongyang to realize that the phenomena are very closely akin. There is in both cases an extraordinary manifestation of power; people are convinced of their sins by another force than reason, and the power that convinces gives them strength not only to overcome sin but to convince others. The Koreans who were at the original meeting have gone forth, like Wesley's converts, their preaching has been wonderfully successful – so much so that there are not a few who say that it is through Korea that light of Christianity will shine to the Far Eastern world.[12]

The Pyongyang revival movement is called the Korean Pentecost. They experienced the mighty power of the Holy Spirit similar to the Pentecost in the book of the Acts. On that night several hundreds of people sat down in the Bible studies to pray, waiting for the mighty presence of the Holy Spirit. William Blair who witnessed the revival meeting described it as follows:

> Every sin a human being can commit was publicly confessed that night, pale and trembling with emotion, in agony of mind and body, guilty souls standing in the white light of that judgment, saw themselves as God saw them. Their sins rose up in all their vileness, till shame and grief and self-loathing took complete possession; pride was driven out, the face of men forgotten. Looking up to heaven, to Jesus whom they had betrayed, they smote themselves and cried out with bitter wailing: Lord, cause us not away forever![13]

The effects of the 1907 revival were very significant for Korean churches. The Christian churches experienced the powerful gifts of the Holy Spirit and Korean Christians realized that true faith in Jesus begins with repentance. It provided spiritual vitality to the churches, it led to campaigns for evangelization for the nation and later mission movements sending missionaries to Jeju island and Manchuria.

Respecting Native Culture

While the missionaries did not want to have confrontation with native Korean religions, their theology of religion was that of the separation model that only Christianity contains the absolute truth that can save sinners. The first Korean Methodist missionary, Horace G. Appenzeller, criticized ancestral worship as a stronghold to be destroyed. He argued that Shamanism produced feelings of fear and social tension among the people. Influenced by the missionaries, many Korean Christians condemned Confucianism as the reason for the downfall of the nation.

The early missionaries did not compromise with the traditional culture. However, they acknowledged that there were some affinities between Korean culture and the Old Testament. They respected Korean culture, but they were very critical of the Korean religions. Many Presbyterian missionaries were graduates of most conservative McComick Theological Seminary and moderate conservative Presbyterian Princeton Theological Seminary; we know that these seminaries theologically did not study and teach about evil spirits, demons, and ghosts, or "the neglected Middles" as defined by Dr. Paul Hiebert, cultural anthropologist. The neglected middles are those between God and man, needing Shamans (*Mudang* in Korean) to drive away evil demons. Dr. Nevius, Princeton graduate, wrote *Demon Possession* translated in Korean. He became deeply aware that in China and Korea this is very important for evangelism, because there are still many men and women possessed by demons in Asia. We read concerning this in Acts 19: 13-16:

> Some Jews who went around driving out evil spirits tried to invoke the name of the Lord Jesus over those who were demon-possessed. They would say, "In the name of the Jesus whom Paul preaches, I command you to come out." Seven sons of Sceva, a Jewish chief priest, were doing this. One day the evil spirit answered them, "Jesus I know, and Paul I know about, but who are you?" Then the man who had the evil spirit jumped on them and overpowered them all. He gave them such a beating that they ran out of the house naked and bleeding.

Many missionaries took the same stance as Nevius on other religions. They were very considerate in judging or condemning Korean religions. Rufus Anderson committed the serious error of identifying Christianity with western civilization in Hawaii, which resulted in ignoring the native culture to which the Gospel was being presented. Henry Venn and John Nevius made much progress by showing a deep concern for the native culture rather than ignoring it. Nevius put an emphasis on self-support, but he also attempted to make the gospel relevant to the native mind. In this sense, Nevius deserves to be called the originator of indigenization. Paik defined self-support itself as indigenization in saying that self-support was "the cornerstone of the indigenization" of the Korean church. Some liberal theologians agreed that the early missionaries had been concerned about Nevius's impact on Korean customs and practices. Underwood wrote in his book, *Summary of the Holy Doctrine,* that the object of introducing Christianity into Korea was not to westernize Korea by means of Christianity. The missionaries highly recommended the use of native Korean architectural patterns in church buildings. Nevius emphasized that missions are not to teach mechanics and civil engineering or foreign languages or science; missions is not to Christianize a heathen land by civilizing them, as some plainly assert, but to Christianize them, and leave them to develop their own form of civilization.

The missionaries left decisions to the judgment of the Koreans in the sensitive issues of alcohol drinking, cigarette smoking and ancestral worship. The Korean Church has a tradition of criminalizing alcohol and cigarettes, which was decided by Korean believers, not by missionaries. Dr. Gale compares the judgment of indigenous cultures and customs to a dog's protection of the house. On sensitive issues such as ancestral rites in this way, the missionary says, "Know it, but don't touch it."

In 1896, one missionary asked a Korean Christian for their opinions on the ancestral memorial ceremony. The answer was uniformly a refusal to offer sacrifices saying that Koreans should remember their parents, but it was common belief that offering sacrifices to dead parents was foolish. Later, a Korean intellectual harshly criticized the Korean church for banning ancestral rites in the 1920s, saying, "It is wrong for the Korean church to ban them, and the ban on ancestral rites is due to the ignorance and self-righteousness of missionaries." He was not an evangelical Christian.

Conservative Theology

The strict Reformed theologians in the West do not like the term "conservative," instead they prefer the term "Reformed." However, this term also can give negative image of narrow-minded Presbyterian and Reformed circles. The primary goal of the Reformation is "Back to the Bible." Accordingly, the reformed faith and theology imply biblical faith and theology. The Presbyterian Council stated that "the Presbyterian churches are holding to the Reformed faith and Presbyterian government," meaning that Korean Presbyterian churches would inherit the Scottish Presbyterianism and the Puritan ethics of keeping the Sabbath day holy. The Council adopted the Westminster Standards of Westminster Confession of Faith, and the Large Catechism and the Small Catechism which were formulated in England 1554. Later in Western Church history, Westminster Confession of Faith was criticized as lacking the doctrine of the Holy Spirit and Missions; because of this, in 1980 the Kosin Presbyterian Churches to which the writer belongs added two chapters of the Doctrine of the Holy Spirit and Missions. Our Confession of Westminster consists of 35 chapters.

The Korean Presbyterian Church was already conservative and Calvinistic when it started. Many theologians do not hesitate to define the theology of the Korean Presbyterian churches as Christian fundamentalism. But Dr. Peter Beyerhaus, an evangelical theologian in Tubingen University in German, is negative towards the early Presbyterian theology, arguing that the theology of the Korean Presbyterian churches is not reformed doctrines, but biblical fundamentalism because of their leaders' confessional tradition. The Presbyterian leaders' confessional tradition is only the Westminster Confession. His criticism on the Korean Presbyterian theology and Churches, we suppose, comes from the Lutheran background. We see in his theology some difference between German evangelical theology and American evangelical theology.[14] Christian fundamentalism denotes a negative image of "exclusiveness, narrow-mindedness and arrogance," however we want to affirm our theological position on Christian fundamentalism as being compatible with reformed theology. The writer graduated from Westminster Theological Seminary which separated from Princeton Theological Seminary in 1929 on the hot theological issue of fundamentalist and modernist debates during the 1920s. Westminster seminary is fundamentalist school, but in America nobody blames Westminster of being a fundamentalist school. We do not deny that there are many fundamentalist Churches and groups giving negative images.

The Presbyterian missionaries started Pyongyang Presbyterian Seminary in 1902, and at that time most missionary professors were strong Calvinists. The representative missionary professors, Dr. Samuel Moffett and Allen Clark, and Dr. W. D. Reynolds were strong Calvinists who learned "Old Princeton theology" in America. In the 1920s, the Princeton Theological Seminary turned to liberalism, so the Reformed theologians such as Gresham Machen, Cornelius Van Til, left the school and established Westminster Theological Seminary in 1929 from which I graduated. We call the Princeton Seminary before the 1920s the "Old Princeton."

The Presbyterian missionaries who came to Korea were not all conservative, because the Australian and Canadian Presbyterian Churches were under the impact of liberal theology. The Australian and Canadian churches sent their missionaries to Korea, so the three senior missionaries professor thought that the Canadian and Australian Presbyterian churches were already under the impact of liberal theology, they carefully checked the theology of the two Presbyterian missionaries, before they performed certain ecclesiastical functions in the Korean church. It indicates that there was a conservative-liberal split in Korean Presbyterian churches from the beginning.

Another route of liberalism into the Korean church was through theological institutions and Christian universities in Japan. Japan was an allied nation with Germany during the 1930s and the 1940s, so the Japanese churches became captive to liberal German theology. The pastors educated in Japan were pro-Japan and they compromised with the Shinto Shrine worship. They did not consider the Shinto Shrine participation a grave sin which the Bible severely condemns. It eventually helped them to support the Shinto nationalism that the Japanese government pursued. Their attitudes are entirely different from the conservative American missionaries and pastors: The Southern Presbyterian missionaries refused Shinto shrine participation and went back to America.

The Korean Presbyterian Church, which emphasizes Covenant theology, has faced difficult tests in the issue of Shinto Shrine worship. When Japan occupied Korea in 1910, they imposed their state religion of Shintoism on the society as well as the churches. The churches in Japan generally compromised with the Japanese government by accepting the Emperor as divine. Only a few Christians and church leaders bravely refused participating in the shrine worship.

The General Assembly meeting of the Korean Presbyterian Church in 1938 made a most shameful decision that Shinto shrine participation is not idol worship, but a national rite ceremony. The venue was surrounded by hundreds of Japanese police officers. The Chairman should have decided on an important issue by voting.

However, the chairman omitted the vote due to pressure from the Japanese police. In the assembly meeting a young American missionary Bruce Hunt attended as a full member. He only appealed to the chairman by raising his right hand, said "Why did you not ask the" No." Immediately 4 Japanese policemen arrested him to put into the Pyongyang prison. This brought serious aftereffects on the Korean church after the Korean liberation from the Japanese occupation in 1945.

Korea was highly receptive to Protestant Christianity and to Roman Catholicism, however, Japan and China rejected Christianity as a Western religion and accepted only Western sciences and technology. Korea changed her image from a hermit nation to permit nation. Christianity was associated with modernization and anti-Japanese colonialism. Because of that Christianity was able to avoid the accusation of being a Western religion. The message, theology, unity among missionaries, and the mission strategy of the three self-formulas can still become the model of churches and missions in Asian where Christianity remains a minority religion. Christians, as well as Korean society, acknowledge the contributions of Christian missions to the nation and society. Those who criticize Korean church growth, theology, and Nevius strategy are liberal theologians who do not agree with evangelical Christianity.

Endnotes

[1] Michael Breen. *The New Koreans: the business, history and people of South Korea* (New York: St. Matin's Press. 2017), 155.

[2] Spencer J. Palmer, *Korea and Christianity: The Problem of Identification with Tradition* (Seoul: Hollym Co., 1967), 15.

[3] A. J. Brown, *The Mastery of the Far East* (New York: Charles Scribner's Sons, 1919), 540.

[4] The Edinburgh Report 1, *Report of Commission 1: Carrying the Gospel to all the Non-Christian World* (New York: Fleming H. Revell, 1910), 78.

[5] Bruce F. Hunt, "Beachhead in Korea," *The Presbyterian Guardian*, January 25, 1960:19.

[6] Charles A. Clark, *The Nevius Plan for Mission* (Seoul: Christian Literature Society, 1937), 19.

[7] Lillias H. Underwood, *Underwood of Korea* (New York: Fleming H. Revell, 1918), 237.

[8] James E. Orr, *Evangelical Awakenings in Eastern Asia* (Minneapolis: Bethany Fellowship, 1975), 30.

[9] Charles A. Clark, 58.

[10] Charles A. Clark, 86.

[11] K. S. Latourette, *History of Expansion of Christianity*, vol. 5, (New York: Harper and Brothers, 1944), 425.

[12] Samuel H. Moffett, *The Christians of Korea* (New York: Friendship Press, 1962), 52.

[13] William Blair &Bruce Hunt. *The Korean Pentecost* (Edinburgh: The Banner of Truth Trust, 1977), 78.

[14] Peter Beyerhaus *Die Selbstaendigkeit der jungen Kirchen als missionarischen Problem* (Wuppertal-Barmen: Verlag der Rheinischen Missions-Gesellschaft, 1956), 254-57.

Chapter - 7

Theological Confrontation in Korean Church

Splits of Korean Church

The Shinto Shrine issue during the Japanese occupation resulted in the churches splitting after the liberation. The first separation of the Presbyterian Church took place in 1952 due to the Shinto shrine issue. Christians and many church leaders who refused to participate in Shinto Shrine worship were put into prison or suffered a martyr's death. Unfortunately, most churches in Korea succumbed to Shinto worship. The division took place in 1952 between those who compromised and those who fought against Shinto nationalism in the Presbyterian Churches.

The next division of the Presbyterian churches resulted from the controversy of biblical criticism debates. Dr. Chai Choon Kim, a representative liberal Presbyterian theologian, taught people to deny Moses' authorship of the Pentateuch in the Chosen Seminary. Many students appealed to the General Assembly in protest against Dr. Km's theology. At that time Dr. Hyung Yong Park, a representative conservative Presbyterian theologian, strongly stood against him. He claimed that his teaching was liberal theology and should not be accepted by the churches. There were exactly 51 conservative representatives in the General Assembly and only 46 liberal representatives to contest them at the legal General Assembly in 1951. After hot debates on that issue, the General Assembly decided to agree with the conservative Park' side. It resulted in the second split among the Presbyterian churches with a liberal Presbyterian group, the so-called *Kijang* Presbyterian Church, left the General Assembly in 1953.

In 1959 the mainline Presbyterian churches broke into two groups of *Hap Tong* Presbyterian and *Tong Hap* Presbyterian due to the membership of WCC. The former strongly resisted joining the WCC, while the latter supported joining the WCC. The terms *Hap Dong* and *Tong Hap* means uniting together in Korean language. Several radical leaders of the *Hap Dong* condemned the *Tong Hap* churches as pro-Communist. The *Tong Hap* group responded to them as being narrow-mined, arrogant separatists.

Theological Challenges of Korean Church

After the Korean liberation in 1945, overseas church leaders, especially the WCC leaders and progressive theologians, began to criticize the theology of Korean Christianity as too narrow and extremely conservative. It indicates that the organization of the WCC in 1948 serves as a challenge to conservative Korean churches. Many world church leaders and theologians visited Japan and Korea. However, some liberal theologians were not welcomed for their criticisms on traditional churches and theology. By my information, Emil Bruner's doctrine of ecclesiology (distinction between the Church and *ecclesia*) and John Hick's pluralism met with severe opposition from relatively open-minded Japanese churches leaders and professor.[1] In Korea, Brunner's denial of Adam as God's creation greatly disappointed many Korean Christians (in 1949).

The General Assembly of the Presbyterian Church in the United States (PCUS) investigated the Korean Presbyterian Church in 1953 and commented that "the theology of the Korean Church is much narrower, more literalistic and intolerant than that of our own Church."[2] John Coventry Smith, the former Chairman of the WCC, also made critical remarks on Korean theology in 1961. He said that "such extreme conservatism led to separation and isolation from other streams even within the Reformed tradition."[3] Conservative thinking was accused of isolating the Church from any knowledge of liberal theology, of extreme confinement to one stream of thought, and of unwillingness to open the doors of the church to liberalism. These criticisms seem to have a measure of truth. It is an undeniable fact that the Korean Church gave the impression to the liberal church that they had reduced all Christian teachings to a series of doctrines. In reference to this point, H. Durr, a Swiss theologian, also expressed his deep concern about the "fundamentalistic contradiction of understanding of the Bible and lack of its relevancy to the present situation"[4] However, Durr was concerned that the Korean churches had the weakness of reducing Christian religion into several specific doctrines. He also highly praised the vitality of the Korean Churches. Unfortunately, liberalism overlooks the Church of Christ as a supernatural and spiritual community. What is the true and genuine doctrine for the Church? Christian theology needs to be faithful to the word of God and to be relevant in the context of the local church. Such criticisms come partly from the different views of Scripture.

Neo-Orthodox Theology in Korea

After the Second World War, liberal Western theology began to enter Korea. It greatly affected the Korean church in negative ways. The new theology resulted in the division of the churches. The WCC divided the major denominations into Presbyterian,

Methodist and Holiness Churches (Korea Evangelical Church) into the pro-WCC and anti-WCC churches. Neo-orthodox theology still divides professors and students within one school into pro-Barthian and anti-Barthian. The impact of Barth's theology was so strong that those who follow Neo-Orthodox theology were being called Barthian. Neo-Orthodox and Barthian became almost synonymous in Korean churches. Neo-Orthodox theology, which arose and developed between the First and the Second World Wars, was introduced to Korea in the late 1930s. *Evangelical Dictionary of Theology* defines Neo-Orthodox theology as follows: "It began in the crisis associated with the disillusionment following World War I, with a rejection of Protestant scholasticism, and with a denial of the Protestant liberal movement that had stressed accommodation of Christianity to Western science and culture, the immanence of God, and the progressive improvement of humankind."[5]

The neo-orthodox theology could be relevant to Korea which had also undergone World War II and the Korean War. This theology attempted to give theological answers to the Europeans who suffered horrible tragedies in the wars. Oswald Spengler condemned the First World War as the *Downfall of the Occident* (the title of his book). Neo-orthodox theology applied existentialist philosophy to their theological studies focusing on the issues of the existence of God and the meaning of human life. Emil Brunner gave a lecture on existentialism in a Japanese Christian university in 1953. The writer spent much time reading during the early 1960s in books almost of existentialism: *Either/Or* by Sören Kierkegaard, *The Strangers* by Jean Paul Sartre; Albert Camus; and *Thus Spoke Zarathustra* by Fredrich Nietzsche. At the same time, cultic groups of the Messianism and the Apocalypse appeared in mushroom phenomena confusing the churches. Korea was in a time of confusion and chaos. In such a context, the names of the theologians Karl Barth, Emil Brunner, Paul Tillich and Reinhold Niebuhr have been widely known in Korean churches. Even some intellectuals of other faiths know them. Among them Barth and Brunner were two giant theologians in the Western world from the 1930s until the 1960s. If the former is a lion on the mountain, the latter is a whale of the sea," was said to be spoken by Karl Barth. These two giants had hot debates *Ya und Nein* (Yes and No) on natural revelation during the Nazi regime. Later it evolved into a relationship of friendly enmity (freundschaftliche Feindschaft) and hostile friend (feindliche Freundschaft), although both were Swiss-born and German theologians. Natural revelation became a hot debating issue between these two theologians: Brunner considered Hitler to be the messiah to save Germany based on natural revelation, while Barth condemned Hitler as "a prelude of Satan's coming." Barth denied the theology of natural revelation. The relation of both theologians was tense theologically. Nevertheless, as Brunner was near to his death, Barth wrote to him as follows: Unfortunately, our relationship has been dominated too much by negativity– playing off the word *nein*. But I want to affirm you, as our Lord has affirmed us–"For the Son of God, Jesus Christ, who was preached by us and Silas and Timothy, was not "Yes" and "No," but in him it has always been "Yes" (2 Corinthians 1:19). "That is my last word to you." In the hospital Dr. Brunner read it, smiled, and died.[6]

The rhetoric and theological words of neo-orthodox theology confused those who study theology, because this new theology's terminology is almost the same with that of traditional orthodox theology. Is the new theology the same as traditional orthodox theology, or not? The conservative theologians expected the Neo-orthodox theology to be theologically orthodox because they have been much dissatisfied with liberal theology which denies the authority of the Bible. Dr. Park Hyoung Yong, a leading conservative theologian, suggested to invite Dr. Brunner to his conservative Presbyterian Seminary, but some American missionaries strongly advised him not to invite him. At that time Dr. Park already wrote an article attacking Barth theology, but it seemed that he did not know about Brunner's theology.

Emil Brunner came to Korea in 1949 after visiting Japan. He visited Japan again and stayed almost 2 years to lecture at Tokyo International University and many other schools. He also lectured to missionary groups and church leaders. In Japan he was criticized by the leaders and pastors of the denominational churches, especially *Kyoudan Church* (United Churches) which was a union of several denominations. He highly praised the *Mukyokai* Church (non-Church movement) which has greatly affected the churches in Japan because of the influence of the founding leader Uchimaura Kanzo. He downplayed the *Kyoudan* Churches (organized churches). His doctrine of the Church idealized *ecclesia* (church) in the New Testament claiming that *ecclesia* is the only pure Christian church that Jesus Christ intended to establish, on the other hand, the Church is historically organized and institutionalized by a Christian community lacking originality and purity. His lectures immediately met with opposition from the denomination churches leader and pastors.

A similar thing happened in Korea. He was invited by Yonse Christian University to give a special lecture. Following his lecture, a young Christian raised a question about Adam. "Dr Brunner, what do you think of Adam? He replied: "Sorry, I do not know from which monkey Adam belongs." These words disappointed evangelical Christians who expecting Brunner at least to be orthodox theologian. Barth and Brunner read the Bible as pastors and theologians, but their interpretation of the Bible turned out differently from the traditional perception of the Bible. Although Brunner re-emphasized the centrality of Christ, evangelical and fundamentalist theologians have usually rejected Brunner's other teachings. Included were his dismissal of certain miraculous elements within the scriptures and his questioning of the usefulness of the doctrine of the inspiration of the Bible. Alister E. McGrath made a critical remark on Brunner that Brunner's reading of the Scriptures could be shallow. It should also be noted that Brunner denied the virgin birth, seeing it as a later doctrinal development which detracted from the true humanity of Christ.

We will examine Barth's theology from a critical perspective. Korean Evangelical Theological Society came to the conclusion in a theological conference that his soteriology is a neo-universalism that everyone has already been saved in Jesus Christ whether or not one believes in Jesus as the Savior. John Hesselink commented Barth as follows: "Barth maintains that the proper object of theological reflection is not the relation of God in religious experience as in Schleiermacher but the relation of God to humanity in Jesus Christ. Against the experientialism and subjectivism that have dominated theological scene since Schleiermacher, Barth is adamant that the basis of faith lies outside of ourselves in God's self-revelation in Jesus Christ. "Our salvation, he argued, has already been enacted and fulfilled for all humankind in God's reconciling work in Jesus Christ. What remains is for us to recognize this fact and live according to it."[7]

Barth emphasizes the mission of the Church, but his concept of mission is entirely different from the traditional concept of mission. His missionary idea is that the purpose of preaching is not to save the lost soul from hell but to proclaim that man was already saved in Christ.

We quote again Hesselink:

Consequently, says Barth, it is not the mandate of the church to call to a decision for salvation, since salvation already extends to them because of Christ's redemptive work on the cross; instead we should call hearers to a decision for obedience. The response that is expected of those who hear the Gospel is basically ethical rather than soteriological in significance.[8]

For Barth, a conversion experience is not important. He denies the believer's experience of the Holy Spirit through the Words of God. The biblical foundation of his neo-universalism is Romans 5:12: "Therefore, just as sin entered the world through one man, and death through sin, and in this way, death came to all people, because all sinned." Accordingly, Barth denied the existence of the hell. In 1963 Barth gave a special lecture in a Chicago seminary in America. At that time, Dr. Edward Carnell, the president of Fuller Theological Seminary, attended the seminar. After the lecture, Dr. Carnell challenged Barth by asking a sensitive question – "Sir, do you believe in hell?" Barth replied, "I believe in Christ, not hell." Barth himself stated that he did not believe in hell as follows: "We believe in Eternal Life, not in Eternal Hell. It is not out of kindness or out of good nature that the Creed does not mention hell and eternal death. But the Creed discusses only things which are objects of faith. We do not have to believe in hell and in eternal death"[9] Barth's incarnational theology has greatly affected Korean churches, for his incarnational theology is that Jesus Christ emptied himself to become a man in order to serve man: "Who, being in the very nature God, did not consider equality with God something to be used to his own advantage; rather, he made himself nothing by taking the very nature of a servant, being made in human likeness" (Phil. 2:6-7). His incarnational theology has been applied to liberation theology and the Minjung theology. Minjung theology is only Korean version of liberation theology. Similarly, Emil Brunner maintains almost the same thought in rejecting Calvin's predestination. Brunner argues that "while scriptures do include an element of reprobation or non-election, these are not eternal decrees like election. Election may be eternal, but non-election is not, according to the scripture."[10] He explicitly denies eternal perdition for the non-elect or the evil ones.

Indigenization Debates during the 1960s

Modern missions have much interest in indigenization. Since the Jerusalem Conference, many discussions have taken place regarding this issue. The indigenization theologians define indigenization as self-adjustment or self-transformation of transcendental truth into the historical situation. They seem to emphasize the revelation of Christ and the Gospel, but they deny the absolute truth claims of Christianity and deny the objective truth of the Scriptures. Their hermeneutic approach was based on the historical criticism of the Bible.

We evangelicals agree that the Gospel message, ministry, church government, and worship need proper application to social and cultural situations. At present, evangelical theology and missions still explore indigenization and contextualization. In fact, the Korean churches are practicing indigenization in church building, worship style, church governance, and theological education. The Korean churches developed a layman preacher being called evangelist which is different in Ephesian 4:11. Strictly speaking, he is simply a Bible teacher or a lay preacher. As far as the church building is concerned, they built church buildings in an indigenous style without receiving money from missionaries. Up to the end of World War II, most Korean church buildings were of a simple native construction, built by local congregations using their own concept, materials and skills.

However, the indigenization discussions in liberal theology have basically arisen from the assumption that the churches in the mission fields smack of "foreignness" or Westernization. Their basic assumption is that Christianity is the products of the revelation of Judaism and the Graeco-Roman culture and philosophy with which evangelical theology do not agree. The Korean Christians are strongly convinced that the fundamental Christian teachings and doctrine we believe are truly biblical. They believe that our Christian Church is built upon the foundation of the Apostles and the Prophets.

Regretfully, liberal theologians and professors claim that the Korean churches and their theology have been copied from the West. The debates of indigenization seemed to have climaxed in the 1960s. The Korean people were everywhere using terms as "nationalism, national consciousness and national-selfhood." This indicated that the indigenization debates came along with the rising of nationalism at that time. The WCC theology and theologians greatly encouraged these debates. On August 27, 1962, D. T. Niles of Ceylon visited Korea and spoke on indigenization at the Christian Literature Society in Seoul. He called for the necessity of a Korean theology. He used the following simile: "First, the Gospel is the seed, the Church is a flower grown from the seed. Then the flowers that come from seed differ according to the soil in which they are grown. Second, the Gospel is theology. There is German theology, English theology in England, Indian theology in India. Likewise, The Korean church should have its own theology."[11]

We evangelicals do not agree with this assumption because the Church of Christ is universal, so theology also should be universal by which the God's covenant people share together commonality and unity in Christ, with some slight differences.

There is only application of the Gospel to the context in which God's people live. The substance of human being is the same beyond time and place.

Conservative professors generally objected to indigenization theology. The indigenization discussions of the liberalists are only theological combination of Korea's traditional thought, Christianity and Western theology. Some gave too much nationalistic flavor and others expressed optimistic view of all components of Korean culture. They do not seriously consider the sinfulness of fallen man in culture and religions. They fail to see the negative functions of other religions. Their more serious theological pitfall is the belief that revelation is even available today in every culture and religion. Evangelical theology recognizes a partial truth and good in other religions and culture, Calvin defines it the seeds of truth. J. H. Bavinck acknowledges "moment of truth in non-Christian religions.[12] His idea comes from the theology of common grace that God's grace extends to both the believers and the unbelievers: "He causes his sun to rise on the evil and the good and sends rain on the righteous and the unrighteous" (Matt.5:45).

Minjung Theology during the 1970s

If indigenization theology was the big issue in the Korean churches in the 1960s, Minjung theology became the hot issue in 1970s. The indigenization debates were largely confined to the Church, but, Minjung theology has become a controversial issue in society as well as in the church. During the 1970s the WCC expressed deep concern on the authoritative regimes and governments in Asia. The Fifth Assembly of the WCC at Nairobi stated it as follows: "In many parts of Asia today, authoritarian forms of government are being established. There is martial law in the Philippines and Taiwan: military rule in Bangladesh; emergency rule in Korea and

India; one party state in the People's Republic of China, North Korea, Vietnam, Cambodia, and Laos. These governments violate human rights in the name of economic development or national security, we believe it poses serious questions about the mission of the Church. We therefore urge the churches to work for the rights of fuller participation of the people of Asia in their own development."[13]

Korea was no exception to this. The tensions between the Korean government and the anti-government struggles can be described as confrontation between the nationalism (particularism) of the Korean government and the WCC's universalism. "Minjung" is a Korean word for people in English. In Minjung theology the term signifies an oppressed people in society. In this regard, Minjung theology is liberation theology contextualized in the Korean Churches. As a matter of fact, it started by Chi Ha Kim, a young Roman Catholic poet. Some claim that he coined the term "Minjung" to describe a fighting by the people against an authoritative government. Gutierrez's *liberation theology* has been translated into Korean by a Roman Catholic theologian. It has become a forbidden book during the military regime. Chi Ha Kim came to be familiar with *liberation theology* of Gutierrez as well as other liberation theologians of Latin America while he was in the jail.

From 1973 onward, Jurgen Moltmann's theology of hope and the WCC's liberation theology were introduced into the Protestants churches in Korea. Some theologians and professors began to discuss liberation theology. Moltmanns's books have been translated into Korean. Several theologians and church leaders participated in the Nairobi Assembly to appeal to the WCC for human rights issue. The WCC expressed its solidarity with Christians of South Korea. In 1975 the four delegates from the

WCC completed a four day visit to Korea and expressed their deep concern over "growing government attacks on churches and church leaders."[14] .

Minjung theology has become first "doing theology" in the Korean churches. Many were motivated to establish the Messianic Kingdom on this world. Their concept of the Messianic Kingdom is only a utopia which is to be achieved through the efforts of men in their struggles for social justice. For them "the realization of social justice is mission and believes the corporate salvation of society is more important than any form of individual salvation."[15] Bonhoeffer who involved in the assassination of Hitler and was subsequently executed himself became a model for Korean Christians to follow. In this way Jesus was idealized since he suffered martyrdom as a political offender.

Inevitably, this politicized theology was met with strong opposition and criticism from conservative theologians. Minjung theologians interpret the Scriptures from political, social, and economic perspectives to the neglect of the spiritual dimension of the Scriptures. For example, a representative Minjung theologian identifies the God's covenant people as poor, oppressed, alienated, and exploited people. Minjung theology "sees the Kingdom of God as a concrete and real world where justice and the love of God would actualize in real life situations."[16]

This writer also wrote many articles and books on this subject with public speeches in seminars and meetings. I also once experienced a hard time because of negatively mentioning the "military revolution" (the military coup d'état by the president Park). He also denounced Minjung theology as radical political theology. Minjung theology as radical political theology neglects the spiritual dimension of human being and eternal dimensions such as the heaven and hell. Minjung theology only seriously consider physical, material, and natural dimension of human beings.

Minjung theologians justified their fighting against the military regime by quoting John Calvin's resistance theory. But this is a serious misunderstanding and distortion of John Calvin. The resistance that John Calvin stood strongly for was not against political pressure but fighting for religious freedom. Dr. Robert McCune, a grandson of senior American missionary, McCune, who refused Shinto Shrine worship and closed the schools, rightly points out: "What, in Calvin's mind justified resistance? One can sum up his answer in just one word: idolatry. If a government permits or even commands idolatry, it must be resisted. If a government misbehaves in other ways, it normally cannot be resisted."[17] Minjung theology regretfully distorts Calvin's resistance theory.

We need to realize that Liberation theology and Minjung theology, even though they claim to be the Third world theology, cannot be applied to the Third world country such as Colombia, Indonesia, India, Philippines, Cambodia, and Vietnam. Some missionaries have been expelled from the country as soon as they taught it. Liberation theology is like pouring gasoline on a house that is on fire. Liberation theology is committed to a sort of secular eschatology. Along with it is a hope that a Utopia will be built on the earth by unaided man. It makes no distinction between the Kingdom of God now and the Kingdom of God to come when Jesus Christ returns. The Nairobi Assembly was sadly silent on such themes as the wrath of God and the final judgment.

Asia needs liberation from Asian religion. The TIME magazine article vividly described more than 150 million Dalits who want to be liberated from the unjust caste system of Hinduism.[18] An Indonesian theologian correctly pointed out that in Asia, religion functions to perpetuate poverty and oppression..[19] The WCC does not make voices on the violations of human rights and religious freedom in the Communistic nations and the Islamic nations. That is the same in Korea. Minjung theologians and the Christian left-groups are silent on the violations of human rights of North Korea, while they are too much critical of it in South Korea. They apply and practice double-standards of human value systems. Finally, it is important to notice that later, Christian radical groups have had an ideological alliance with the left- wing groups and the pro-North Korean communists; continue their campaign against the conservatives, Christian churches, and conservative government. Here the conservative denotes the people and social movements who are ideologically holding to capitalism and democracy.

The Pluralism Debates during the 1990s

Theology of religious pluralism claims that every religion can reach to the same "ultimate Reality" or salvation. Accordingly, it denies the absolute truth claim of Christianity.[20] In Korea, pluralistic theology, by and large, is not welcomed because, as Hick recognized, "a strongly evangelical form of Christianity flourishes" in Korea.[21] But we need to define plurality and pluralism. Plurality means the peaceful coexistence of every religion in society and nation. Pluralism as theology claims that every religion is equal before God. Democratic society of the West is equalizing even religion and ideology. This idea basically comes from the relativistic atmosphere of the Western theology and philosophy. We see a theological contrast between the Asia and the West. In Asia some radical religionists attempt to realize theocracy on their nation based on a kind of militant absolutism. At the same time the West seems moving toward relativism denying the absoluteness of Christianity.

As early as the 1980s, a few pluralists began to introduce a theology of religious pluralism into the Korean churches. In the early 1990s it had become a controversial issue, especially in the Methodist churches. Evangelical Methodists responded by strongly reaffirming the traditional exclusivist model of salvation. Because of the ensuing theological controversy, some were worried that the Methodist churches would suffer an unfortunate division. However, the controversy has not caused a division yet, although the gap between the two positions has further widened. Eventually the Methodist Church committee excommunicated two pluralists, concluding that their theology was syncretistic relativism.

The pluralists in Korea have been influenced largely by the Western pluralist such as John Hick and Paul Knitter. We need to mention a Methodist woman professor of theology who has emerged as a well-known female theologian because of her controversial keynote address, entitled "Come Holy Spirit--Renew the Whole Creation," presented at the WCC's Canberra Assembly held February 7-20, 1991. Her address has drawn severe criticism from evangelicals in Korea. We did not think that her view does not represent the Third World theology, nor even Christian women in Asia. She syncretized the Christian concept of the Holy Spirit with the "spirits" of Korean Shamanism. A Western missiologist offered the following comments on her presentation: She orchestrated a "happening" that dramatically interwove her theology of the Holy Spirit with the issue of creation, indigenous peoples, other faiths and non-Western cultures.[22]

In the WCC assembly, the Greek Orthodox and Evangelical participants expressed their deep concern over her keynote address as follows: "We must guard against a tendency to substitute a private spirit, the spirit of the world or other spirits for the Holy Spirit who proceeds from the Father and rests in the Son."[23] Here we need to notice pluralism theology from the Asian perspective. Most Asian evangelicals are greatly disappointed with the Western pluralism which is promulgated in the non-Western world while the Western churches continue to undertake missionary work there as a top priority. The Asian church's disappointment with John Hick's pluralism is seen in a Japanese theologian's complaint to Hick when he visited Japan in the 1980s. It is reported that a neo-orthodox theologian criticized Hick at the welcoming party for him. The Japanese leader pointed out that Hick's pluralism makes it difficult for Japanese churches to survive in Japan as a small minority because it elevates each religion to a level equal to Christianity.[24] This critique indicates that not only evangelicals but a significant number of neo-orthodox and liberal theologians in Asia question the principles of pluralism. Nevertheless, pluralism is well received in Asia by the students of comparative religion and some radical Protestant theologians. Pluralism theology challenges evangelicals to theologically develop evangelical theology of religion. And we must notice that most people in Asia prefer pluralist model of salvation to exclusivism model.

We can summarize the evangelical's criticism on pluralism as follows: First, religious pluralism may be a new idea for some Western theologians, but many Asians have always been exposed to pluralism, because many think instinctively that all religions lead to an ultimate reality.

Second, this kind of Western pluralism has only served to frustrate and disappoint Christians and lower the status of the Christian church further down which is only at best a minority religious community surrounded by oppressive religions and cultures of other faiths. Paradoxically, at the same time, Western pluralism has elevated the status of these non-Christian religions to the level of Christian religion.

Third, John Hick seems to concentrate only on the view that each religion is a legitimate response to the ultimate reality which they claim to reach. Many people in Asia, however, are not so much concerned with the metaphysical aspects of religion as they use their religion to meet their own felt needs, such as solving health problems, poverty, and using it to become a success in business or in social life. The struggle for political power is a major factor in the religious resurgence movements, so that their promoters are not so interested in the metaphysical aspects of religion.

Fourth, pluralists misunderstand the term "exclusivism," which is used mainly by evangelicals. Pluralists interpret this term as a symbol of arrogance, superiority, and bigotry. However, the term "exclusivism" is a theological, not a sociological concept. This means that, sociologically, Asian Christians who are being persecuted as followers of a minority religion cannot express or encourage an arrogant, superior attitude toward their neighbours. Theologically, the terms "absolutism," or "exclusivism," should be understood in the light of the absolute claims of the founder of Christianity, Jesus Christ, who said that he alone is the way of salvation and the revealed truth (John 14:6). In this regard, Jesus Christ is the only Saviour, excluding all others.

Fifth, pluralism does not adequately answer the negative aspects of other religions under which many Asians are suffering and from which they would like to be liberated. Asian evangelicals would like to make a comparative analysis of the moral impact which these religions exercise on their societies where they dominate. Finally, other religions also claim that they are true. Thus, their claims to be the exclusive way of salvation also contradict Hick's claims.

It is often said that "daughter churches" are more conservative than "mother churches." This phenomenon has proven to be true in Korea. American conservative missionaries taught Biblical conservatism to the Korean Churches, but unfortunately, liberal theologians who deny the inspiration and infallibility of the Scriptures sharply charge conservative Christian as being arrogant, exclusivist, legalistic, and other worldliness. The Korean church has never doubted the inspiration and inerrancy of the Scripture upon which Christianity is founded. Accordingly, they consider that denying the authenticity of the Scripture is tantamount to denying genuine Christian identity.

We believe that healthy and responsible exclusivist absolutism in Christianity is the source of spiritual conviction, courage, and comfort for persecuted Christians. It contributes to spiritual vitality, which in turn is expressed in affection and services toward neighbors whatever their religion. We want to advocate a sensitive, loving and wise expression of Christian exclusivist. And we need to respect the people of other religions, upholding the principle of unrestricted liberty regarding religions. Neo-orthodox theologians and liberal theologians advocate the Heaven without the Hell. They need to listen to the warning words of R. Rheinhold Niebuhr who is also known as neo-orthodox theologian: "A God without wrath brought men without sin into a Kingdom without judgment through ministration without the cross."[25]

The liberalists and the left-wing groups need to realize that social transformation is impossible without individual regeneration; it has been proved in Korean politics. Every new government attempted to do campaign for social and national reform. Nevertheless, it never resulted in success as expected. At present, contexts-oriented liberalism seems to be losing its dynamic and relevance in Korea churches. Why?

Finally, we close this chapter by quoting Dr. Gresham Machen who devoted all his life for the defence of biblical Christianity: "Liberalism on the one hand and the religion of the historic church on the other are not two varieties of the same religion, but two distinct religions proceeding from altogether separate roots."[26]

Endnotes

[1] Concerning the visits of Emil Brunner to Japan, John Hesselink, "Encounter in Japan: Emil Brunner An Interpretation," https://repository.westernsem.edu/pkp/index.php/rr/article/download/27/33/.

[2] John Coventry Smith, "Policy Lessons from Korea," International Review of Missions Vol 50 (1960): 322.

[3] John Coventry Smith, 322.

[4] H. Durr, "Einiges aus der Missions-Gescichte Korea," *Evangelisches Mission Magazine* .vol. 9:4 (1950): 14.

[5] R. V. Schnuckur, "Neo-orthodoxy," in *Evangelical Dictionary of Theology*, ed., Walter A. Elwell, 819.

[6] I. John Hesselink, "Karl Barth and Emil Brunner – A Tangled Tale with a Happy Ending," in *How Karl Bath Changed My Mind*, ed., Donald K. McKim, (Grand Rapids: Eerdmans, 1980), 131-32.

[7] I. John Hesselink, 128.

[8] I. John Hesselink, 128.

[9] https://postbarthian.com/2015/05/22/karl-barth-believe-eternal-life-not-eternal-hell.

[10] http://www.sdmorrison.org/double-predestination-is-unbiblical-email-brunner.

[11] D. T. Niles, "The Bible Study and Indigenization," *The Church and Mission Korea*, ed., Harold S. Hong, (Seould: CLSK, 1963), 279-80.

[12] J. H. Bavinck, *An Introduction to Science of Missions*, tr. David H. Freeman, (Phillipsburg: Presbyterian and Reformed Pub., 1960), 228.

[13] David M. Paton, ed., *Breaking Barriers: Nairobi 1975* (Chicago: Moody Bible Institute, 1975), 98.

[14] Ho Jin Jun, "A Critical Study of the Impact of Ecumenical Theology on the Korean Churches," (Dissertation of Doctor of Missiology presented to School of World Mission, Fuller Theological Seminary in 1979), 296-97.

[15] Jun, "The Tangun, 270-71.

[16] Sang Bok Lee, *A Comparative Study Between Minjung Theology and Reformed Theology form a Missiological Perspective* (New York: Peter Lang, 1996), 144.

[17] Robert McCune Kingdon, "Calvin and Calvinists n Resistance to Government," (unpublished paper presented in International Congress on Calvin Research, August 27, 1998), 5.

[18] Tim McGirk, "India's Untouchable Are Mounting a Rebellion against Upper-Caste Privilege Their Weapon Are Educaton," *TIME*, October 20, 1997: 19.

[19] A. A. Yewango, *Theologia Crucis in Asia* (Amsterdam: Rodopi, 1987), 75.

[20] Concerning pluralism theology, refers to Ho Jin Jun, *Religious Pluralism and Fundamentalism in Asia* (Colorado Springfield: International Academic Pub., 2002) Chapter. 3 and 4.

[21] John Hick, *Christian Theology of Religions* (Louisville: Westminster John Knox Press, 1995), 117.

[22] David Kerr, "From Christology to Pneumatology," *International Bulletin of Missionary Research*, 15: 3 (July 1991): 102.

[23] David Kerr, 102-3.

[24] Dr. Harold Netland had attended the party for John Hick as a missionary in Japan. .

[25] H. Richard Niebuhr, *The Kingdom of God in America* (Chicago: 1937), 193. Recited from Mark Lilla, *Stillborn God*, 248.

[26] Gresham Machen, *Christianity and Liberalism* (Grand Rapids: Eerdmans, 2009), 27.

Chapter - 8

Liberation from Religion: Present Korean Religions

From Chaos to Stability

Korea experienced chaos and disorder after World War II and the Civil War (1950). However, in the course of time Korea settled down gradually to progress from chaos to stability in society, politics, and economy. After liberation, the Republic of Korea was built on the Constitutions of Democratic Republic based capitalistic free society. However, Korean Peninsula was divided into the North and the South, so Korea has become the first victim nation of the Cold War between the East and the West. First chaos came from the tensions between the right-wing groups pursuing free democratic nation and the left wing attempting to establish communistic nations.

Before the liberation there were more Christians in North Korea than in South Korea, and immediately after the division of North and South, many Christians moved to the South for freedom of faith. They actively joined the right-wing group to fight the left-wing groups and communists in the South. Still, Korean society is undergoing ideological tensions and conflicts between two groups, regrettably many Christians support the left wings groups and political party which are anti-Christian, anti-capitalist, anti-democratic; it indicates that the Christian churches are negatively changing from the early churches by the impacts of liberal theology and the WCC.

In the early 1960 two "revolutions" of the 1960's Demonstrations and the military coup d'etat took placed; The "April Revolution" in 1960, was a popular uprising led by labor and student groups, which overthrew the autocratic First Republic of South Korea under Syngman Rhee. It led to the resignation of Rhee and the transition to the Second Republic of South Korea.

The May 16 military coup d'état 1961 led by military general Park Jung Hee and his allies rendered powerless the democratically elected government of the Second Republic, and later Park become president of the ROK through the election. One year before the coup, it was a time of great social and political unrest.

"The coup was instrumental in bringing to power a new developmentalist elite and in laying the foundations for the rapid industrialization of South Korea under Park›s leadership, but its legacy is controversial for the suppression of democracy and civil liberties it entailed." The military leaders termed it the «May 16 Military Revolution» and assumed to be «a new, mature national debut of spirit», the people including the writer did not like the term "Revolution;" at that time the most people have been worried about the future of the nation. The 1960s and 1970s of Korea was the age of the confrontation between the military regimes and the antimilitant protesters whose opponents widely ranged from students, professors, military men, and many Christians. This issue will be discussed in the section of liberation; however, it is to be noticed that this military government have surprisingly contributed to the rapid economic and industrial development of the nation, the professors of political scientist defined it as "development dictator." Many dictator rulers in Asia justify their authoritative ruling in the name of national security and economic development, but it has been almost failed. In this respect the Park's dictatorship has become the model in Asia. Even still the left-wing groups are accusing him of dictator, while the conservative people and many Christians highly respected him as "dictator for the country;" he was not involved in any kind of corruption.

Despite social crisis and ideological conflicts, Korea has achieved economic and industrial development in the short period of time, and it helped the Korean churches to become a missionary sending nation in the grace of God. It should be attributed to ideologically capitalism, democracy and Christianity. When Korean missionaries were kidnapped by Talibans in Afghanistan in summer 2007, the *Economist* magazine politely criticized both the Taliban as well as the Korean missions their aggressive mission works, and made a very significant comments on Korean Christianity as follows: "Initially embraced in the early 20th century as a means of asserting Korean identity against Shinto Japan and Buddhist China, Christianity is now a symbol of status, and, along with capitalism and democracy, part of an ideological trinity enthusiastically adopted from the West." (August 2nd, 2007). The report explicitly implies that Korea has achieved economic and industrial progress by democracy, capitalism, and Christianity.

Samuel Huntington also remarked in his book *the Clash of Civilization* that he compared Korea with Ghana, saying that sixty years ago, Ghana and Korea received the same amount of aid from the U.S. at a similar level, but Ghana has become a poor country and Korea has become a donor country. From the late 1980s many international economists and the international political scientists began to study the so-called the 5 tigers nations of Japan, South Korea, Singapore, and Hong Kong, Taiwan in order to explore the reasons for the economic progress which are especially occurring in the nations of Confucianism; they attempted to see it in the values system of Confucianism, claiming that Confucian value system can become the alternatives to Max Weber's assumption in Asia.

Interactions of Religions

Korea has no state religion, official religion, and dominate religion functioning as communal and national solidarity; it represents that Korea has no religion or culture that unifies the nation, society, and culture with invisible binding force. The major religions of Buddhism, Confucianism, the Roman Catholic and the Protestants are relatively peacefully coexisting as a religious plural society. Religious plurality is demonstrated in the fact that both Christ's and Buddha's birthdays are national holidays. Still, within many Korean Christian family circles there may be adherents of Confucianism or Buddhism. On a Sunday morning the son and daughter may go to the church while the mother or grandmother may go to the Buddhist temple. The father might practice the tradition and culture of Confucianism in his daily life. Even the highly educated young secular generation might go to the Shaman to have their fortune tellers.

Three major religions of Buddhism, Confucianism and Christianity have undergone "correlation" or "the fusion of horizon" in which religions maintain reciprocal relations by influencing each other in positive ways. For instance, Korean Buddhism adopted from Christianity some forms of worship, religious education, religious organization, and missionary methods. Before they did not have worship or rituals on Sundays, but nowadays they have Sunday worship services. Plus, they have erected Buddhist temples in the cities, whereas Buddhism has usually been called "the religion on the mountain."

When the chaplains of Protestant churches in Korea developed mass baptismal ceremonies equivalent to the mass conversion movement into Christian churches in India, Buddhism and Roman Catholic churches also adopted this to the degree of mission competition. Buddhist chaplains (monk) who have had contact with Christian chaplains have played a leading role in Buddhism's contextualization.

Confucianism in Korea has no priests or temples and even no registration for their adherents. Confucianism is not missionary religion, so they don't know about mission or evangelism, however, they are striving to increase their impact on society through propagation of Confucianism. Confucianists are seeking to strengthen and revive their religion in order to make a contribution to national development through social reform. They have begun to publish Confucianist magazines in order to spread the teachings of Confucius, thinking that only Confucianism can cure the morally and spiritually diseased society. They have founded small Confucianist schools in every province and towns, and organized youth and women's groups; they organized Confucian student groups on the university campuses, through which they aim to propagate Confucianism.

An Indian professor who researched the Independence Movement of the Korean churches of the 1910s and 1920s told me that Gandhi's ideology for his independence movement is indebted to the nationalism of the Korean churches. Is it too much to say that Gandhi's reinterpretation of Hinduism was profoundly influenced by Christianity and Western civilization? He "was a Hindu who politely rejected the dogmatic claims of Christianity while embracing, with every ounce of his will, the ethical claims of Christ." Some critics accused him of being a "secret Christian." From Gandhi's experience and others, we see that Christianity has radically influenced Asian religions and religious leaders; they have modified some of the objectionable elements in their religions and borrowed ideas from Christianity, to make them more relevant to modern society. Gandhi is no exception in this respect.

Resurgence of Religions

Korean religions experienced resurgences during the 1970s and 1980s. Christianity experienced remarkable growth in terms of numbers, and the resurgence of other religions are partly the result of social conditions that people are not satisfied with a society becoming too materialistic or individuals losing true humanity from urbanization and industrialization. Religions are a "resource for those seeking to answer questions beyond the scope of science and technology and looking for a depth of experience that may be missing from everyday life."[1]

However, there is a big difference between Christian revival and resurgence of other religions: Christian revival is based on individual's experience of the Holy Spirit, but the other religion's revival or resurgence lacks individual's faith experience of their god or ultimate Reality (Buddhism), rather it is the fruit of the work of religious elite or leaders to achieve their own religious or political purpose.

In other Asian nations people tend to have serious cultural identity crisis and they seek to resolve it in their cultural heritage and religion. It is the same in Korea. Such a religious resurgence tends to strengthen their dominant religion, while they attempt to exclude minority religions from their community. Ninian Koshy, who has served for many years on the staff of the WCC's Commission of the Churches on International Affairs, has rightly pointed out that the religious revivals in Asia challenge pluralism and often result in discrimination against minority religions, but that did not happen in Korea. The religious resurgence of Confucianism, Buddhism and nationalistic indigenous religion resulted in increasing tensions and conflicts between religions. Concerning the conflicts between Christianity and Confucianism, it goes back to the old history when Christianity came to Korea. The major issue was the ancestral worship in which committed Christians refused to participate in it. My family has passed through this persecution, but it will continuously be a challenge for Korean Christians.

In Korea there was tension between Christianity and nationalistic indigenous religions. Recently the *Tangun* religion, which rests on the myth that three gods founded Korea as a nation, started a campaign to erect the statue of *Tangun*, a founder of the nation, in about 300 primary schools around the nation. Not only do they worship *Tangun* as national god, but also encourage schools to teach it to pupils. They argue that the *Tangun* religion is the only absolute religion and Christianity is an imported religion so Christianity should be excluded from Korean society. According to them, all the religions including Christianity and Buddhism, and all human races whether white, yellow, or black have originated from these Korean national gods.[2] To such a campaign some radical Christians responded by destroying or damaging *Tangun* statue during the night and it eventually led to physical violence between Christians and adherents of the *Tangun* religion in some cities. Christian churches protest and appeal to the government to stop the campaign in the demonstrations.

Buddhism is the oldest and one of the largest religions in South Korea, but until 1972 no official statistics were available concerning the number of its adherents. Buddhism experienced remarkable numerical growth during 1970s and 1980s. Although Buddhism has many temples and priests, its organizational structure had not developed as much as that of Christianity. Buddhism learned missions from Christianity and began to actively engage in evangelism. A Buddhist leader in South Korea said that, "propagation is the life of the human, as bread is the life of the human." Buddhism strengthens its expansion work by sending missionaries to the East as well as to the West. The Won Buddhism which is contextualized new Buddhism, borrowed much ideas from Christianity in administration, system, and worship. Their University attracted many students from the around nation.

Mainline Buddhism has changed from "Buddhism in the mountains" to urban Buddhism, by planting small and large temples in cities, and by developing various programs to appeal to young people and intellectuals. Political Buddhists have recently protested against the Government's religious and social policies; they are even attempting to gain political power by helping many Buddhists to be elected in the national General Election. Until the early 1980s, the Government had always supported Buddhism in South Korea, but this has been changed. Since 1983, "Minjung" (people) Buddhism emerged; it advocates the political and social involvement of Buddhists. Buddhists have contextualized their rituals, worship, organizations and ceremonies. They admit that they have learned much from Christianity in this respect. They are actively propagating their religion through literature, education, and social activities; they have also begun to attack Christianity by printing a number of books and other materials in which they openly condemn or criticize Christianity. In South Korea efforts at dialogue between Buddhism and Christianity have been made occasionally due to the initiatives of liberal Protestant theologians and Roman Catholic Church leaders.

The tensions between Buddhism and Christianity have been growing during the 1990s: A Buddhist journalist argues that in South Korea Christianity has ignited a kind of religious war due to its animated missionary movement, and its arrogant, exclusivist attitude toward Buddhism. The South Korean army is a typical location for tension between the two religions. Roman Catholic, Protestant and Buddhist chaplains compete to win soldiers to their respective religions. In particular, the conversions of some Buddhist priests to Christianity and their anti-Buddhist literature and sermons, have created even more tensions and conflict between the two religions. Buddhists feel deeply disappointed and angry that South Korean Christians condemn Buddhism as a religion of idolatry belonging to "Satan." Some radical Christians, sadly, destroyed Buddhist signs and symbols in public places and streets. Such aggressive action by extreme Christians has incited South Korean Buddhists against some Buddhist leaders declaring a "religious war."

The anti-Christian feelings among Buddhists was very intense and serious, because one Protestant chaplain moved an image of Buddha installed in his army camp to the corner. It brought about strong complains and protest from Buddhism chaplains; so, the Headquarter of the Army chaplains arranged the seminar to peacefully settle down. The Headquarter arranged 3 professors respectively from Protestant, Buddhism, and Catholic, among them the writer was chosen representing the Protestant. It was October in 1998. Two speakers from Buddhism and Catholic respectively targeted the Protestants' exclusivist and aggressive evangelism as the cause for the conflict. The writer as final speaker responded to them and Buddhism and Catholic chaplains by asking a question, "Do you not believe your religion as absolute truth?" I emphasized that every religion claims exclusive truth and salvation, however, theological exclusive claim and social exclusivism claim should be separated: socially exclusivist attitude should be blamed, but the adherent to any religion should not be forced to abandon their faith as absolute truth. I suggested to make a distinction between social exclusivism and doctrinal exclusivism.

Again, I challenged them by taking out the issue of persecution of dominate religion on Christians in Sri Lanka. If Protestant exclusivism becomes a main factor for religious tension in the army and society, how can we explain the religious clashes occurring in Hinduism, Buddhism and Islamic countries, and why are only Christians persecuted in Asia. After my lecture, a Buddhist chaplain commented that the persecution in Sri Lanka by Buddhists is a kind of retaliation to Western colonialism, not against Christians. I was told that the meeting was very helpful in understanding each other

Conflicts between religions become more intense in the election for president and national congress. They compete fiercely the politicians of their religion to be elected. Especially in presidential election they do not have a Buddhist presidential candidate, while Christian presidential candidate is likely to be elected, they are more nervous. That was the time of presidential election in 1992. The Government had arranged the meeting for the purpose of promoting harmony and peace between religions, because Buddhists were unhappy with the predominance of Christian candidates for the Presidency. At the meeting a Buddhist leader strongly charged Christians of being too proud and exclusivist especially towards Buddhists. Korea has freedom of religion, but

Christian exclusivism are always the target of blame and accusation from other religion.

Value System Debates

In 1985 an Institute in Germany convened academic conference in the theme of "21st Century: Asian Century," in which Confucian value system was highlighted as plausible theory explaining the rapid economic growth in Japan, Hong Kong, Singapore Taiwan, and South Korea; The Western economists in the conference gave their much emphasis to Confucian value system, claiming that Confucianism has become an alternatives to the Max Weber's assumption. Herman Kahn refers to these nations as "neo-Confucian cultures" with a Confucian ethic. John Hick highly praises them, saying that "Buddhist-Shinto Japan is not poor or technologically backward, and several other non-Christian nations of the Pacific Rim are also rapidly becoming major industrial powers."[3]

Against the suggestions, Korean professor Park Woo Hee refuted it contending that the worldview of Confucianism teaching the harmony of human beings with nature cannot bring about economic progress, Confucianism as state religion in the Yi Dynasty for 500 years has failed to reconstruct the nation; rather, Confucianism has become hindrances to industrialization and science.[4] We suppose that this conference perhaps would have ignited the value system debates in Asia on the relation between and economic development and religion. In addition to this Samuel Huntington's "the Clashes of Civilization" spurred more the debates; Dr. Huntington came to Korea with the invitation from Kim Dae Jung, the leader of the opposition political party. After that, some Confucian scholars began to claim that Confucian value system has contributed to the economic growth in South Korea.

Some Asian economists argue that the economic and industrial development of these countries confirm the potential of the Confucian tradition. They challenge Max Weber's hypothesis that only the ethics of Protestantism can create capitalism. For example, a South Korean economist contends that the Confucian ethic may have been an important factor in economic growth in South Korea. According to him, the value system of Confucianism such as the family and human relation oriented social system, respect for education, hard work, diligence, self-discipline, absence of religious or ideological constraints inhibiting the pragmatic pursuit of ends, all made contribution to economic development in South Korea.[5] To this claim a professor who majored in Chinese culture and religion in Taiwan wrote a book entitled *Confucius Should Die; Nation Can Survive*,[6] in which he severely criticized Confucianism for negatively impacting Korean culture and society. However, his book has been severely responded with hot criticism from the pro- Confucianism scholars. Nevertheless, his book has been a best seller in South Korea in the late 1990s.

After the financial crisis in 1988, Confucianism has been blamed for the financial crisis in South Korea. A critic of Confucianism claimed that Confucianism is "a cause of Korea's downfall during the modern era."[7] For example, Confucianism and its family-oriented value system resulted in "collective egoism" family, community and social organizations gave excessive preference to their own group's interests, at the expense of national or public interests. Other critics also had the same viewpoint that human relations and "familism" exclude the hiring of specialists in business world, and this can be seen even in the Korean churches.

Many Korean economists agree that Weber is correct to say that Confucianism, Hinduism, and Buddhism have not been conducive to economic prosperity, although Confucians stress on hierarchical family relationships which has influenced Japanese industry. This prosperity, it is claimed, springs from the sense of vocational calling in Protestantism, every job or profession is holy to God; so, there is no dichotomy between "sacred work" and "secular work." However, Asians tend to evade "menial jobs" such as digging ditches, farming, and mining; instead the occupations of clergy, academia, and government service are preferred, as they are thought of as "holy works."

A Japanese-American political scientist Fukuyama asserted that South Korean familism has become a crucial factor in the failures of the conglomerates, in which family as owners are involved in business. Often these families make irrational decisions by neglecting advice from specialists. The reason for excluding specialists in business are due to the lack of mutual trust found in Korean society. Consequently, the owner trusts only his family.[8]

As to the impact of Confucianism on South Korea in the past, an Asian political scientist writes, "The introduction of Confucianism to Korea only made the *yangbans* (noble class) more arrogantly contemptuous of everyone beneath them. They took to the idea of leisure and avoided all forms of exertion as though these were the accepted prerogatives of the aristocracy."[9] Despite the faults inherent in Confucianism, the cultural conservatives attempt to defend Confucianism. Modernization and the prominent presence of Korean churches in society inevitably resulted in calling the reactions from the nationalists and cultural conservatives: they have paid attention to the "forgotten religion" because of their deep concern that modernization may have resulted in the loss of cultural identity and true morality. Some nationalists attempted to defend as the last fortress of national morality.

Although Confucianism strenuously efforts for its recovery and revival, our society seems not to give much attention to it.

Confucianism still has many limitations to attract people into their religion. Capitalism further required persons willing to deny themselves rationally and systematical for the sake of achieving a future goal. The dominant strain of Protestantism (e.g., Calvinism, Puritanism, Pietism, Anabaptism) produced such qualities because of its inner-worldly asceticism, encouraging members to be active "in the world" - indeed, to prove their salvation by their socioeconomic actions. At the same time, these forms of Protestantism expected their members to forgo the 'pleasures of the world' - not to spend money on luxuries, drink, gambling, or entertainment. Protestant ethic therefore became one of hard works, sobriety, financial care, and deferred gratification. Even though capitalistic gain was far from the goal of these Protestant values, according to Weber, the initial development of capitalism was made possible by the available pool of persons who shared these qualities.

Now in Korea Confucian value system is facing critical crisis, for the young generation already abandoned the Confucian ethics emphasizing loyal to nation, honoring parents and elders, commitment to extended family and community; they become too much individualistic. Even though the young generation do not adopt Christian value system, they, without much hesitancy, accepts secularism as a by-product of Western civilization. Nevertheless, many university students go to the fortune-teller asking for their future destiny.

Shamanization of Korean Religions

All the Asian religions were syncretized with animism (shamanism), Korea is not an exception. Shamanism (animism) is mainly preoccupied with healing, exorcism, meeting man's felt needs, participation in rituals, ceremonies and meditation; so, individual's transformation in character can hardly be expected. Shamanism has had no moral principles or precepts urging people to change and become new persons. The low level of morality among the Asian people is manifested in every aspect of society in politics, government, economy, education, the military, and elsewhere. Catholic theologian Hans Kung strongly condemns it as follows: Superstition claims absolute authority for (and blind obedience to) something which is relative and not absolute; it worships either a material thing or a human person or a human organization.

Buddhism in Korea has been syncretized with shamanism, so, the experience of ultimate Reality is confined to a few professional Buddhists. Their main interests are, in most cases, focused on achieving their desires through prayers and magic. The transcendental experience is an important religious issue only for professional and devout Buddhists. For example, South Korean Buddhists, like many Christians, have been so secularized that they have little concern for the transcendental world. Many Buddhism monks are engaging in healing ministry like some Christian church pastor and pray for 100 days for the women who cannot bear children. Of course, they receive money from the woman concerned.

In the Korean churches the convergence between Christianity and shamanism has become most prominent features in the Pentecostal churches. The Full Gospel Church of Rev.Yong Ki Cho is a most prominent. This is the largest congregation in the world. During the 3 decades of the '60's, '70's, and '80's, the Korean churches recorded a remarkable growth in terms of numbers. The "mushroom" phenomenon of church growth seems to be ascribed to "Shamanized messages" of the pastors focusing on this-world oriented blessing and prosperity.

Prosperity theology or prosperity gospel is a belief that financial blessing and physical well-being are the will of God. Rev. Cho preached a Korean version of the prosperity gospel, which taught that "leading a prayerful lifestyle will bring rewards not only in terms of health, but in wealth. Still, prosperity theology and blessing theology coined by Cho has dominated   the Korean churches. The powerful messages of blessings and healing ministry attracted huge numbers of people from all parts of Korea and the church accumulated huge amounts of money and property. It represents that the messages fulfilled the felt needs of the poor people; the Church grew rapidly during the 1970s when the society was economically in a poor situation. Rev. Cho stated that his messages basically focused on giving bread to the poor and healing the sick, the bread is replaced by blessing from God and healing the sick is replaced by the healing ministry through laying of hands on the body.

However, this theology is subjected to criticism by many theologians and evangelical ministers. Jesus preached that believers should suffer for the sake of his Kingdom. Blessing theology downgrades noble spiritual truths and God's blessings into money and health. Unfortunately, the recent money scandals of the Church have negatively damaged the Korean churches. It is said that many young people are leaving the Church. The rapid economic growth of the society no longer necessitates prosperity theology of the Churches.

From the above explanations, we learn that Korean religion failed to do social responsibility by being too preoccupied with individual blessing due to the religion becoming shamanized. With regard to this, Dr. Byung Kook Kim gave meaningful advices to the Korean religions including Christianity that the Korean religions neglect the supernatural dimensions of religions, so they have failed to provide the great future goal toward which Korean politics and society should aim at; They should have made strong voices against politics as politics go in wrong direction; the religions must strive to maintain their orthodox doctrines against heresies; and the spiritual realms should be priority to the secular realms, but the Korean religions became too much preoccupied with earthly gains from the politics. He argues:

> The religions of Korea neither fought among themselves as orthodox as orthodox and heresies, nor joined force together against their common 'enemy,' the state, along the line of the secular *versus* the spiritual. Religions were strictly a matter of individual preference to be practiced in homes, monasteries, and churches with the objective of gaining the personal fortunes in this earthly life. And such a role identity of religions prevented the spiritual and secular realms. Of human life from being in a direct confrontational relationship.10

The close contacts of the religions may lead to mutual understanding as well as competition. Religious competition is not desirable, but there is constructive competition in religion. Constructive competition of religions is the source of religious and social development, and it helps religion developing self-awareness and reforming themselves, so that they may make effective efforts to adapt to new situations. On the other hand, destructive competition can contribute to conflicts and war of religions. The three major religions in Korea are characterized by tensions, constructive competition, and often cooperation for communal peace and national interests when the nation face critical crisis. Korean Christians suffer still some tension from ancestral worship; some Christians participate in ancestral worship thinking that it is cultural accommodation, while evangelical Christians consider it to be compromising with idol worship.

Korea, which became the first victim of the Cold War, experienced extreme confusion, poverty and corruption. As early as the 1950s, Korea was the poorest country in the world. In the 1960s, it was a country that received aid from Southeast Asian countries. During the 1960s Cambodia was more advanced nation than South Korea. However, the economy and industry rapidly developed and has become one of the OECD nations.

Korea has a pluralistic society with no state religion, no official religion, and no dominating religion. In three Kingdoms Dynasties and subsequent Koryo (Korea) Dynasty, Buddhism controlled the nation and in the Yi Dynasty Confucianism dominated the nation and society, in the age of Japanese occupation, people were spiritually under the control of Shintoism. Liberation in 1945 was a liberation from spiritual control of religion, past-oriented, anti-reform tradition and culture. Westernization, modernization, and Christianity came together to Korea, so, people never consider Christianity as a Western religion. Some international mass media reported that capitalism, democracy, and Christianity played a great role in economic progress in Korea.

In 2002, the Pew Global Research Center in the United States conducted a survey research the relationship between religion and economic development in 44 countries. It has concluded that a country with a state or dominant religion is economically poor. In Korea religion is not a communal choice but an individual choice.

Unfortunately, the religions of Korea are syncretized with shamanism so, it is said that every religion fails to transform society and nation. Even Christianity is not exempted from this criticism, shamanism has had no moral principles or precepts urging people to change and become new persons. Confucianism advocates loyalty to one's country, self-discipline, and becoming a person of virtue, charity, and love for one's neighbors, but this does not lead to individual transformation. Confucianism uses the term "virtue," but it does not teach inner transformation of the individual. It rather teaches that the human beings have the potential to become good humans.

Christianity demands theologically the inner change of person. A German missiologist Horst Rzepcoski properly pointed out that Christianity looks to the future and demands the change of person. Christianity take seriously the new man as their goal. The notion of a new man, a new earth, and a new heaven imparts to history the stimulation and impulse for national development and advancement.[11]

Endnotes

[1] Julia Day Howell, "Religion," in *Culture and Society in the Asia-Pacific*, eds., Richard Maidment and Colin Mackerrans (London Open University. 1998) 139.

[2] Chang-Bum An, *The Through of God and the Origin of Buddhism* (Seoul: Samyang Pub., 1994).

[3] John Hick, "The Non-Absoluteness of Christianity," in *The Myth of Christian Uniqueness: Toward a Pluralist Theology of Religions*, eds. John Hick and Paul Knitter, (Maryknoll: Orbis Books, 1987), 24.

[4] Park Woo Hee, "Industrialization and Cultural Identity: with Special Reference to Confucianism in Korea," in *The 21ˢᵗ Century: Asian Century?* eds., Takeshida Ishhara and Park Sung Jo (Berlin: Express, 1985), 96.

[5] Kwan-Suk Lee. "Back to the Basic! New Interpretation of Confucian Values in Korea's Economic Growth." *Korean observer* 26:2 (Summer 1995): 105-106.

[6] Byoung-Yul Choi, *Kongjaka jukeuya, narakasandk (Confucius Should Die, Nation Can Survive)* (Seoul. Hia Pub., 1999).

[7] Bvung-Kook Kim. "Confucian Culture. Party Politics and Democratic Consolidation in Korea: The Anti-Confucian Politics." (paper presented to 15th World Congress of the International Political Science). Association 17-21 August 1997. Seoul Korea). 3.

[8] Francis Fukuyama, *TRUST: The Social Virtues and the Creation of Prosperity* (New York: The Free Press, 1995), 150-54.

[9] Lucian W. Pye, *Asian Power and Politics: The Cultural Dimensions of Authority*, 83.

[10] Byung Kook Kim, "Confucian Culture, Party Politics and Democratic Consolidation in Korea: The Anti-Confucian Confucian Politics," (Unpublished paper in 1998), 18.

[11] Horst Rzepkowski, "Enwiklung und Religion," in *Missions Theologie*, eds., Hans-Werner Genzichen und Horst Rzecepkowski (Frankfurt: Dietrich Reimer Verlag, 1985), 172.

Bibliography

A.A. Yeyangoe. *Theologia Crucis in Asia*. Amsterdam: Rodopy, 1987.

Abraham K.C., ed., *Third World Theologies: Commonalities and Divergencies*, Maryknoll: Orbis Books, 1990.

Andrew Brother. *Battle for Cry*, Old Tappan: Fleming H. Revel, 1997.

Barth, Karl. *Church Dogmatics*. 1/2, trans. G. T. Tompson, Edinburgh: T&T Clark, 1980.

Bavinck, J.H. *An Introduction to Science of Missions*, tr. David H. Freeman. Phillipsburg: Presbyterian and Reformed Pub.,1960.

Beyerhaus, Peter. *Die Selbstaendigkeit der jungenKirchenalsmissionarischen Problem*. Wuppertal-Barmen: Verlag der Rheinischen Missions-Gesellschaft, 1956.

Blair, William & Bruce Hunt. *The Korean Pentecost*, Edinburgh: The Banner of Truth Trust1977.

Bosch David. *Transforming Mission: Paradigm Shift in Theology of Mission*. Marryknoll: Orbis Books, 2008.

Breen, Michael. *The New Koreans: the business, history and people of South Korea* New York: St. Martin's Press. 2017.

Brown, William. *The History of Mission of the Propagation of Christianity among the Heathen since the Reformation*, Philadelphia: Cole 1816.

Brown, A.J. *The Mastery of the Far East*, New York: Charles Scribner's Sons, 1919.

Brown, L. W. *The Indian Christians of St. Thomas: An Account of the Ancient Syrian Church of Malabar*. Cambridge: The University Press, 1956.

Bruce, F. F. *Commentary on the Book of the ACTS*. Grand Rapids: Eerdmans, 1976.

Burkitt, F. Crawford, *Early Eastern Christianity*, London: Gorgias Press, 2004.

Church Missionary Society. *The Missionary Register for M DCCC XVIII*, London: L. B. Seeley, 1818.

Clark, Charles A. *The Nevius Plan for Mission*. Seoul: Christian Literature Society, 1937.

Eckhard, J.Schnabel. *Early Christian Missionary: Paul & The Early Church*. Vol 2, Downers Grove: InterVarsity, 2004.

Elwell, Walter A. *Evangelical Dictionary of Theology*. Grand Rapids: Baker Book House, 2000.

E Graham, Fuller. *A World Without Islam*. New York: Little Brown, 2010.

England, John C. *The Hidden History of Christianity in Asia*. Delhi: ISPCK, 1996.

F. Crawford Burkitt. *Early Eastern Christianity*. London: Gorgias Press, 2004.

Fuller, E Graham. *World Without Islam*. New York: Little Brown, 2010.

Gibbon, Edward. *The Decline and Fall of the Roman Empire*, Herforth Classics, 1989.

Hick, John. *Christian Theology of Religions*. Louisville: Westminster John Knox Press, 1995.

Hodge, Charles. *Systematic Theology*, vol. I, Grand Rapids: Christian Classics Ethereal Library, 2005.

Jun, Ho Jin. *Religious Pluralism and Fundamentalism in Asia*, Colorado Springs: International Academic Pub., 2002.

Latourette, K.S. *A History of Christian Mission in China*, New York: Russell and Russell, 1929.

_____. *History of Expansion of Christianity*, Vol. 5, New York: Harper and Brothers, 1944.

_____. *Introducing Buddhism*. New York: Friendship Press, 1956.

_____. *A History of Christianity*. Vol.2. New York: Harper & Row Brothers, 1970.

Lilla, Mark. *The Stillborn God: Religion, Politics, and the Modern West*, New York: Alfred A. Knopf, 2007.

Machen, Gresham. *Christianity and Liberalism*. Grand Rapids: Eerdmans, 2009.

Moffett, Samuel H. *The Christians of Korea*. New York: Friendship Press, 1962.

_____. *A History of Christianity in Asia*. New York: Harper, 1992.

McGavran, Donald. A. *The Bridges of God.* New York: Friendship Press, 1955.

Neill, Stephen. A *History of Christian Missions.* New York: Penguin Book, 1964.

OoiKeat, Gin and Volke Grabowsky. *Ethnic and Religious Identities and Integration in Southeast Asia,* Chiang Mai: Silkworm Books, 2017.

Orr, James E. *Evangelical Awakening s in Eastern Asia,* Minneapolis: Bethany Fellowship, 1975.

Paton, David M.ed., *Breaking Barriers: Nairobi 1975.* Chicago: Moody Bible Institute, 1975.

Palmer, Spencer J. *Korea and Christianity: The Problem of Identification with Tradition.* Seoul: Hollym Co., 1967.

Paton, David M., ed. *Breaking Barriers: Nairobi 1975.* Chicago: Moody Bible Institute, 1975.

Richardson, Don. *Eternity in Their Hearts,* Venture, California: A Division of Gospel Light, 1981.

Short, Philp. *Pol Pot: The History of a Nightmare,* London: John Murray, 2004.

Speer, Robert E. *Missions and Politics in Asia,* New York: Fleming H. Revell, 1899.

Stavenhagen, Rodolfo. *Ethnic Conflicts and the Nation-State,* New York: St. Martin Press,1996.

Steward, John. *The Story of A Church on Fire.* Edinburgh: T &T Clark, 1928.

The Edinburgh Report 1. *Report of Commission 1: Carrying the Gospel to all the Non- Christian World.* New York: Fleming H. Revell, 1910.

Torrance, Thomas. *Kingdom and Church.* London: Essential Book, 1996.

Underwood, Lillias H. *Underwood of Korea.* New York: Fleming H. Revell, 1918.

Vos, Frits. *Die Religionen Korea,* Berlin: VerlagKohlhammer, n.d.

Vos, Geerhardus. *Biblical Theology: Old and New Testaments,* Grand Rapids: Eerdmans, 1948.

Walker, Williston. *A History of the Christian Church,* New York: Charles Scribner's Son, 1959.

Warneck, Gustav. *Outline of a History of Protestant Missions From the Reformation to the* Present Time. New York: Revell, 1902.

_____. *EvangelischeMissionslehre,* 3 Abt., Friedrich Andreas Perthes, 1903.

Weber, Max. *The Religion of India: The Sociology of Hinduism and Buddhism*, trans, Hans H. Gerth, Glencole: The Free Press, 1960.

Richter, Julius. *Eaangelisches Missionskunde*. Leipzig: Dieterchterische, 1927.

Rodolfo, Stavenhagen. *Ethnic Conflicts and the Nation-State*, New York: St. Martin Press, 1996.

Yohanan, K.P. *Revolution in World Missions*, Lake Mary, Florida: Creation House, 1996.

Korean and Japanese

Choi, Byoung-Yul. *Kongjakajukeuya, narakasandk. (Koean)* (Confucius Should Die, Nation Can Survive). Seoul: Hia Pub., 1999.

Onosizuo, *Nippon Protesutanto Dendousi* (Japanese) (*The Mission History of Japan*) Hirosima: Reformed Church of Japan Pub., 1989

Ranajit, Pal. *Butkyono Mesopotamian Kikigensetz (Japan)* (*The Mesopotamian Origin of Buddhism)*, Osaka: Dongbang Pub., 1995.

Tsmori Nakano. IitaTakamimi, and Yamanaka Hirosi, eds., *Shyukyotonashonalizumu.*(Japan) (Religion and Nationalism). Kyoto: World Thought Pub., 1999.

Watabe Nobuo, *Azia Den Si* (Japan) (The Mission History of Asia) (Inochino Kotoaba, 1999).

Article

Balz Heinrich."Uberwindung der Religionen' und das Ziel der Mission: Die Diskussionzwischen G. Warneck und E. T. Troelztch 1906-1908". in *Es began in Halle*, edsDieter Becker/Andreas Feldtkeller, Heraus, Erlangen: Verlag der Ev.-Luth. Mission, 1997.

Blair. William, & Bruce Hunt. *The Korean Pentecost*. Edinburgh: The Banner of Truth Trust, 1997.

Conn, Harvie M."God's Plan for Church Growth: An Overview," in *Theological Perspectives on Church Growth*, ed., Harvie M. Conn, Nutley, New Jersey: Presbyterian and Reformed Pu, 1976.

Coventry, Smith John. "Policy Lessons from Korea,*" International Review of Missions.* Vol 50, 1960.

Durr, H. "Einigesaus der Missions-Gescichte Korea," *Evangelisches Mission Magazine* vol, 1950.

D.T. Niles."The Bible Study and Indigenization," *The Church and Mission Korea*, ed., Harold S. Hong, Seoul: CLSK, 1963.

Garbe, Richard. "Contributions of Christianity to Buddhism". *The Monist*. April 1912.

Hesselink, I. John. "Karl Barth and Emil Brunner – A Tangled Tale with a Happy Ending," in *How Karl Bath Changed My Mind*, ed., Donald K. McKim. Grand Rapids: Eerdmans, 1980.

Holsten, Von Walter. "Reformation und Mission". *Archiv fur Reformartionsgeschichte* 44, 1953.

Hunt, Bruce F. "Beachhead in Korea," *The Presbyterian Guardian*, January 25, 1960.

Huhtinen, Pekka. "Luter and World Missions: A Review". *Concordia Theological Quarterly 65;1 January 2001*.

Julia, Day Howell. "Religion," *Culture and Society in the Asia-Pacific*, eds., Richard Maidment and Colin Mackerrans. London: Open University, 1998.

Jun, Ho Jin. "*A Critical Study of the Impact of Ecumenical Theology on the Korean Churches*," Dissertation of Doctor of Missiology presented to School of World Mission, Fuller Theological Seminary in 1979.

Kerr, David. "From Christology to Pneumatology," *International Bulletin of Missionary, Research*, 15: 3. July 1991.

Kingdom, Robert McCune."*Calvin and Calvinists n Resistance to Government,*" unpublished paper presented in International Congress on Calvin Research, August 27, 1998.

Kook, Kim Byung. "Confucian Culture, Party Politics and Democratic Consolidation in Korea: *The Anti-Confucian Confucian Politics*," Unpublished paper in 1998.

Langteau, James D., Jun Ho Jin, Gossett Kenneth, and Dna Samora, "Peace Mission to Karen and Shan Migrants from Myanmar in Southeast Asia". *International Journal of Frontier Missiology,3o: 1 Spring, 2019*.

Michael, Nai Chiu Poon. "The History and Development of Theological in South East Asia," in *Handbook of Theological Education in World Christianity*, eds. Dietrich Werner et al. Oxford: Regnum Books International, 2010.

Niles D.T. "The Bible Study and Indigenization". *The Church and Mission Korea*, ed., Harold S. Hong. Seoul: CLSK,1963.

Pierson, Paul. "Nestorian Mission," in *Evangelical Dictionary of World Missions*. Grand Rapids: Baker, 2000.

Schnucker, R. V. "Neo-orthodoxy", in *Evangelical Dictionary of Theology*, *ed*, Walter A. Elwell. Grand Rapids: Baker Academic, 2001.

Smith, John Coventry. "Policy lessons From Korea". *International Review of Missions* Vol 50, 1960.

Yoder, John. "Reformation and Mission: Literature Review". *Occasional Mission Bulletin Journal* 22, 1971.

Tim, McGirk. "India's Untouchable Are Mounting a Rebellion against Upper Caste Privilege. Their Weapon Are Education. *TIME*, October 20, 1997.

Transform World: *Global Challenges Summit 2012*. Unpublished materials presented in Transform World Conference in Bali, November 2012.

Kerr, David. "From Christology to Pneumatology" *International Bulletin of Missionary*. Research, 15:3, July, 1991.

Kingdom, Robert McCune. "Calvin and Calvinists n Resistance to Government". Unpublished paper presented in International Congress on Calvin Research. August 27, 1998.

Knopp, W. "Chrakteristerisches am Missionmotive der Englander". *Allgemeine Missionzeitschrift* 40. 1913.

Internet

"A historical analysis of hindrance related to the slow growth of Christianity in Thailand." http://www.academia.edu/37250138; December 4, 2018.

"Christianity in Pre-Islamic Persia: Latin America Resources," www. Iranionline.org/articles/Christinity-1, 2018.

Concerning the visits of Emil Brunner to Japan, John Hesselink. "Encounter in Japan: Email Brunner An Interpretation". https://repository. westernsm.

Edu/pkp/index.php/rr/article/download/27/33/.

Dr. Zakir Naik."Categorization of Major World Religion," https://www. islam101.com/religion/categoriesofReligion.

Edward, Jason A. "Pol Pot's Little Red Rock". https//socialhistory.org/ news/articles/10993.

Go Duck Duck. "Ancient Greek philophies, Buddha's Philosophy, and Vedic philosophies?" https://www.quora.com/What-are-the-similarities-and-differences-between-the-ancient-Greek-philosophiles-Buddha, 2018.

Gokhale Prasad."Antiquity and Continuity of Indian History" ,1996, www. gaurang.org/indian_phil/prasad_gokhale_indian_history.html

Henri. "The African root of Latin Christianity," www.30giorni.it/articoli_id_3553_13htm. Edward Jason A,"Pol Por's Little Red Rock," https// socialhistory.org/news/article, 1099.

Hesselink, John. https://postbarthian.com/2015/05/22/karl-barth-believe-eternal-life-not-eternal-hell. http://www.sdmorrison.org/double-predestination-is-unbiblical-email-brunner.

Hildebrand, Kelly."A historical analysis of hindrance related to the slow growth of Christianity in Thailand," http://www.academia. edu/37250138, 2018.

Huhtinen, Pekka, 27. https://en.Wikipedia.org/wiki/Martin_Luter_and_anti_semitism. https//heidelblog.net/2014/03/did-luther-calvin-favor-evangelical-monsticism.

Masis, Julie, "Mormons on the March," December 7, 2010. *Asia Times* Online trp://www.atimes.com/atimes/Southeast_Asia/LL07Ae01.html.

Naik, Dr. Zakir. "Categorization of Major World Religion," https://www islam101.com/religion/categoriesofReligion.

Prasad, Gokhale. "Antiquity and Continuity of Indian History", www gaurang.org/indian_phil/prasad_gokhale_indian_history.html. 1996.

Renan, Ernest. https://en.wikipedia.org/wiki/Ernst_Renan: December 10, 2018. http://www.sdmorrison.org/double-predestination-is-unbiblical-email-brunner.

https://postbarthian.com/2015/05/22/karl-barth-believe-eternal-life-not-eternal-hell.

The Syriac Orthodox Church". https://en.wikipedia.org/wiki/Syriac-Orthodox_Church.

Tessier Henri. "The African root of Latin Christianity", www.30giorni.it/articoli_id_3553_13htm.

"What is Christian leadership", https://online.campbellsville.edu/ministry/Christian-leadership-principle.

Winter Ralph. "The Two Structures of God's Redemptive Mission", www. undertheiceberg.com/wp..content/uproad, 2006/4.